T0106089

THE HUNT

a Science Fiction Mystery

TOM WILLISON

authorHOUSE®

AuthorHouse™
1663 Liberty Drive
Bloomington, IN 47403
www.authorhouse.com
Phone: 1-800-839-8640

Published by AuthorHouse 09/16/2013

ISBN: 978-1-4918-1751-3 (sc)
ISBN: 978-1-4918-1750-6 (e)

Library of Congress Control Number: 2013916785

LIST OF CHARACTERS

Steve Gordon—naturalist at Williams Creek State Park

Gerald Pence—CEO of Pence Technology Corporation and developer of the Altair aircraft (XSA)

Janet Taylor—executive secretary to Gerald Pence

Doc Ewing—park labor supervisor and Steve Gordon's boss

Chuck Manning—special agent, FBI Chicago office

Kyle Broyles—special agent, FBI, Indianapolis office

Dan Upstein—executive vice president of Pence Technology Corporation

Daryl Atkins—president and CEO of Porter Aviation Corp

Becky Pence—daughter of Gerald Pence

Darlene Pence—Gerald Pence's wife

Steven Gordon Jr.—older son of Steve Gordon, who attends Indiana University

Robert Gordon—younger son of Steve Gordon, who attends Purdue

Mary Davis—personnel director of Pence Corp

Dean Marshall—legal vice president of Pence Corp

Casey Rodgers—county sheriff and chief investigator for the Indiana State Police

Sergeant Allen Wilson—from District Eight of the Indiana State Police

Homer and Anne Cummins—security people on Pence's farm

Bob Zimmerman and Jason Bonneau—park labor
supervisors reporting to Doc Ewing

Ted Bently—county deputy sheriff

Herb Jennings—district conservation officer, Indiana

Big Man and Little Man—security men for Dan Upstein

Jake—supervisor of Pence's Altair laboratory

Farid Sherazi—student assistant in Pence's Aircraft Lab

Jessica—Steven Jr.'s girlfriend

Agent Kolosky—FBI agent assigned to guard Pence's house

David Berman—Upstein's lawyer

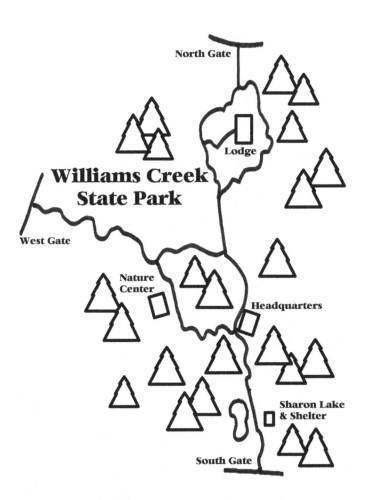

Part One

THE HUNTERS

CHAPTER 1

The board of directors of the Pence Technology Corporation sat around the conference table in the Tylar Nichols Lodge. Gerald Pence, president and CEO, was late.

Bill Chenowith, chief financial officer, tapped his pencil nervously on the table top.

"I'm told he was pretty soused last night. He might be sleeping it off in his room."

Janet Taylor, executive secretary to Pence, was worried.

"I've been up since six, and I haven't seen him anywhere. Hangover or not, he's never been late for a meeting."

"For sure he wouldn't have left the building this morning with those hunters out there," contributed the company personnel director, Mary Davis.

Executive Vice President Dan Upstein, pulling at his graying beard, paced around the small conference room deep in thought. "We'll wait another ten minutes."

He sat down and contemplated the open notebook in front of him. He had never really approved of the idea of holding an informal executive meeting in the Williams Creek State Park in southern Indiana, especially during the period of a scheduled three-day, public deer hunt.

3

This was the third and last day of the hunt, and according to park regulations, they were quarantined to the Tyler Nichols Lodge until five o'clock that evening.

"Why the hell he wanted to meet down here, I'll never know."

Legal vice president, Dean Marshall, made up the fifth member of the group.

"A perfectly good conference room in our building in Indianapolis, and he wants to meet down here in the boondocks!" He continued mockingly.

"He wanted seclusion!" snapped Janet Taylor, her round face reddening.

"Yes, and a place where we might relax and think through our problems," said Chenowith.

"And get our heads blown off by a bunch of wild men with rifles," Dean retorted.

Chenowith leaned toward him.

"Your mind-set is just what we're trying to avoid, Dean. Lighten up! Those 'wild men' will be gone at the end of the day, and besides, there's nothing to do out there at this time of the year anyway. Merry Christmas!"

The others chuckled.

"Something's wrong here. Has anyone asked at the front desk?" inquired Janet.

"I asked the gal to ring his room," Dean responded. "No answer."

"Good God, Dean! He could be lying in there dying from a heart attack or a stroke," Chenowith rebutted. "I'm going to get a key and look!"

Steve Gordon was the park naturalist. His huge six-foot-four frame was jammed into the cab of his van as he supervised the hunters arriving through the main park entrance. The deer kill was not expected to be heavy on this, the final day of the hunt, but considering the first two days, it was anticipated that the overall harvest would be satisfactory.

This was the third deer hunt in four years at Williams Creek State Park. Over the stringent objections of local environmentalists, the hunt was conducted to reduce the excessive deer populations in the park and to restore the balance of foliage for both the deer and other wildlife. That was part of Steve's job. He was trained in resource management at the University of Illinois, where he played linebacker for three years on the Illini football team. He was good, but not enough to play in the pros, so he went on to get his master's Degree at DePauw University in Indiana. It was there that he met and married Carolyn Bates. A year and a half later, Steven Jr., their first son, was born. The Indiana Department of Natural Resources had interviewed Steve earlier and had then hired and assigned him to the Williams Creek Park as its interpretive naturalist. Their second son, Robert, was born a year later. Both Carolyn and Steve agreed that this would be their family.

The radio in his truck blared. It was Doc Ewing, park labor supervisor.

"Steve, we have a problem. There's a guest that can't be located at the lodge and is presumably outside on the grounds. We're going to have to suspend all hunting for the present."

Steve picked up the mic.

"Damn, we've got fourteen already dispersed!"

"Sorry, Steve. We've got to round them up." Steve shook his head. This was going to be a mess.

The desk clerk opened the door of room 126. Gerald Pence was not there.

"Neither bed has been slept in," Chenowith said. He stood by the ground level window that looked out on to the woods to the left and to the lodge's annex to the right. "I can't believe Gerry would wander outside with the hunt going on."

"He could have gone out last night. The hunters weren't there then," Mary Davis said.

"As I've told you all, he wasn't in any condition to be going anywhere," Dan responded.

The desk clerk stood nervously the door.

"There are hunters out there now, and I'm afraid we're going to have to put a stop to everything until Mr. Pence is found," he said.

"Yes-yes, do that for Pete's sake. And call whoever is responsible around here to start a search," Chenowith stuttered.

The clerk rushed off.

Janet couldn't help the tears. She nervously wiped them away.

"I don't understand." She looked the room over. "His suitcase is here; his clothes are hanging in the closet and . . ." She bent over. "And his cell phone is here . . . on the floor between the beds!"

Bill grabbed it from her.

"This is getting more mysterious by the minute." He pressed the 'on' button and read a number in the window. "Does anyone recognize 317-555-3805?"

Janet answered. "That's his unlisted home number!" Then she gasped.

"On the floor . . . where the phone was! Is . . . isn't that . . . blood?"

"And here . . ."

Chenowith held back the left window curtain.

"My God," barked Dean. "It looks like a bullet hole!"

The two park managers, Bob Zimmerman and Jason Bonneau, stood with Steve in front of Doc Ewing's desk in hushed expectation. Ewing's fingers rapped incessantly on the desk top.

"What's this all about, Steve?"

"A group down from Indianapolis for a business conference. One of them, their president, I'm told, is unaccounted for. Didn't show up for a scheduled meeting this morning. He's nowhere in the main Lodge or the annex, and unless he has left the park completely, he's wandering around somewhere outside."

"Why the hell was a conference scheduled down here during the deer hunt anyway?" shot Ewing.

Steve shrugged.

"What about the hunters. Are they under control?" Doc continued.

Bob Zimmerman spoke up. "We can't locate two of them as yet, but we'll get them shortly, I'm sure."

"Okay." Doc stood and reached for his coat.

"Jason, I want you to supervise finding those two hunters. Bob, you find out if those hunters we've accounted for have seen anything. Steve, come with me to the lodge. I'd like to talk to those business people."

As they began filing out of the service building, the county sheriff's car pulled up. Ted Bentley, a ten year deputy sheriff, stuck his head out the window.

"What brings you out this way, Bent?" Ewing inquired.

"Your missing guest," he answered.

"Well, I think we have things pretty well under control," Doc returned.

"It might be worse than you think, Doc. We may have an accident or a kidnapping or a possible homicide on our hands."

"A cell phone found on the floor, blood stains on the rug, and a bullet hole in the window. I'd say we've got quite an assortment of unusual circumstances," voiced Herb Jennings, the district conservation officer for Indiana.

Jennings was seated across from park service personnel and the county sheriff, Casey Rogers, around waning flames in the fireplace on the second floor balcony of the lodge.

"There were also blood drops outside the room and on the steps by the exit toward the Annex," Steve Gordon added.

Herb rose to his feet and stood in front of the fireplace.

"It's almost dark. It makes no sense to continue our search. Let's send the Drew group back until tomorrow."

Camp Drew, a military training reserve, was located north of the park and, under normal circumstances, would supply work crews to give park employees a hand during abnormally heavy daily workloads. In this case they had supplied ten men to help scour the woods during the search.

Herb fed a log into the fire and watched it flame up. "Okay, where are we here?" he asked, returning to his seat.

Doc Ewing spoke up. "The Indianapolis guests have been confined to the lodge until we have a chance for serious conversation. The governor's office has been informed of the situation, and they're sending representatives from state police headquarters down here in the morning. I understand that includes some guys from the crime lab."

"Hell, we don't know if there's been a crime committed," Casey Rogers said.

Doc continued. "I don't know what they'll find of any value in Pence's room. Certainly it won't be fingerprints. Everybody and their mothers have been in there."

"I hate to bring this up," Steve said, "but you know the media people will be swarming all over the place tomorrow, if not sooner."

"My God, I forgot about that." Herb moaned.

"We won't let them past the gates," Doc suggested.

"Hell, we can't do that," Herb retorted. "Lord knows what they'd say about this if we didn't at least give them something. Steve!"

Steve flinched.

"You're the personality guy around here. You handle them if and when they swarm in." Herb smiled at Steve's obvious discomfort.

"Now, back to our guests from Indianapolis." Sheriff Rogers changed direction.

"I'd like to talk to each of them as soon as possible and find out what this is all about."

Steve wanted to look over room 126 before the lab people arrived in the morning, but Sheriff Rogers objected.

"That room is off limits, Steve. You know that."

"I won't touch anything. I'll wear surgical gloves. Indulge me, Casey."

Rogers gave in, and together they slipped under the yellow police tape.

A sports jacket and trousers were neatly hung on the clothes rack. The suitcase lay open below the clothes. It was unpacked, except for the toilet kit which was on the sink in the bathroom. Nothing was out of order.

Neither of the beds appeared to have been slept in, but the one closest to the window had been laid on. The blood stains between the two beds were covered with a towel. With a nod from Casey, Steve lifted the towel and studied the stains. He made no comment as he replaced it. He moved to the window and examined the hole halfway up the left pane. He looked out toward the wooded area across the road from the building.

"What do you think happened here, Casey," Steve inquired as he reexamined the hole.

Casey Rogers was three inches shorter than Steve Gordon, but his stocky frame and thick neck attested to four years of football at Indiana University as a star offensive left guard. His sharp, clean-shaven features and piercing brown eyes belied his fifty-nine years of life. He had majored in Criminology at IU and received his master's degree in that subject during the time he was serving as an apprentice county police officer in Bloomington. He had joined the Williams Creek County Sheriff's Department as a Deputy in 1978, was elected to the position of County Sheriff in 1992, and reelected twice since then leading up to this year—2000. His wife of twenty-one years had presented him with three children—all daughters.

"If we had found a body in here, I would lean toward a stray bullet from one of the hunters. But there's no body. Frankly, I don't know what to think."

Steve leaned toward the punctured window.

"Look at this bullet hole. Do you notice anything peculiar?"

Casey shook his head.

"Look down here." Steve continued, pointing to the sill below. "What do you see?"

"Nothing."

"That's right. If a stray bullet had come in from the outside wouldn't there most likely be glass fragments here?"

Casey scratched his head. "Hey, you're right."

"And I'm betting you'll find those fragments on the ledge outside the window."

Casey studied the brick ledge through the glass. "By God, Steve, you're right. I can see some fragments from here!"

Steve moved to the covered blood and removed the towel once again.

"If Pence had been hit mortally, there would be far more blood on the floor than there is here, and . . ." he said, moving to the wall opposite the window, "if it had been a grazing wound, there would be a bullet lodged somewhere in the wall in this area."

His hand swept over the surface of the wall. Casey approached it and scanned the area closely.

"There's no bullet hole. That means . . ."

"It seems to mean that the weapon was fired through the window from inside this room."

Doc Ewing sat at his desk sipping a cup of coffee. Bob Zimmerman and Jason Bonneau sat quietly opposite him drinking theirs from Styrofoam cups. Doc was staring out the window. It was six forty-five in the morning and still dark. Snow had been forecast for that afternoon—as much as five inches. All we need on top of everything else, Doc thought.

The park had had to cut back on personnel because of the state budget crisis, and any abnormal workload had put a strain on the work crews. "Lean and mean" had been the catch word for the last several years. But as always, they would manage to make do.

Doc was used to managing under adverse circumstances. In Vietnam he had served as an army helicopter pilot from 1968 to 1971. In that time he was shot down twice, received the Purple Heart twice, and was awarded the Bronze Star with Oak Leaf Cluster for meritorious performance of duty under fire. He was honorably discharged in the spring of 1972 and enrolled at Purdue under the GI Bill to study natural resources and environmental science. He graduated in three years and was immediately hired by the Indiana Department of

Natural Resources. Two years later he met and married Nancy Gregory. They had a son, Jon, a year later. That would be their only child because, after three miscarriages in ten years, Nancy died of cancer. The ten year old Jon and Doc, then forty two, never fully recovered from the shock of Nancy's death. Six years later, Doc was hired as Labor Supervisor at the Williams Creek State Park. Seven more years had passed. Doc was now fifty-five, and twenty-three-year-old Jon was serving as a sergeant in the United States Marine Corps stationed at Qauntico, Virginia. Yes, Doc was used to managing the hard stuff.

Steve Gordon's van pulled up outside, and in a moment he joined the group.

"Apparently this situation knows no bounds," Doc said, putting his cup down and leaning toward the group. "First, we're missing a corporate executive, and now we find that two of the fourteen hunters are still unaccounted for."

"We combed the place," Bob Zimmerman pleaded.

"They could have left by one of the other two gates," voiced Jason.

"Not likely. I figure someone would have seen them!" retorted Doc.

"Or they're still here in the park . . . hiding from us," Steve said.

"Hiding from us!? Why the hell would they want to do that, Gordon?" Doc's patience was thinning.

"Because I think they could be involved in Gerald Pence's disappearance."

"Aw, come on, Steve. Don't be so damn dramatic. Why would you say that?"

"It can't all be coincidence," Steve answered. "I think there was a person or persons in Pence's room when whatever happened, happened, and it could mean those two hunters had something to do with it."

"You ought to be a mystery writer, Gordon. You have one hell of an imagination!" Doc mocked.

The phone rang.

"Yeah." He paused to listen. "Okay, we'll be up." Doc hung up and stood and stretched his five-foot-eight frame.

"A Sergeant Wilson and his gang from the state police are up at the lodge. Let's go. And Detective Steve . . . let's do a little more listening and less speculating!"

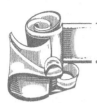

CHAPTER 2

“**W**e manufacture semiconductors, specifically computer chips, for sophisticated corporate systems.”

Dan Upstein's throat was dry and scratchy as he responded to the first question from Doc Ewing. This was one of five simultaneous interviews taking place in the Tyler Nichols Lodge. Dan Upstein was tall and lean and well groomed. His Vandyke was neatly trimmed and helped compensate for a balding pate. His eyes were dark under full gray brows and had an annoying glisten to them. His fingers nervously tapped the arms of his chair as the dark eyes skewed Ewing in mild contempt.

“Do you have any ideas about what's going on here?” Steve Gordon asked, leaning toward Upstein.

“We were here to discuss some serious problems with our company. Pence was worried about these, but I can't believe they had anything to do with him disappearing.”

They were meeting on the balcony above the lobby. Logs had just been added to the fire in the stone fireplace, and the crack and pop sounded over the momentary silence.

“Signs are quite clear, Mr. Upstein, that whatever happened to Mr. Pence involved violence.” Doc continued.

"Could the problems your company is experiencing have anything to do with that?"

The dark stare was getting to him. Upstein waved his hand vigorously. "No, no! I can't believe that it did. Gerald had no enemies that I know of." He rose and walked to the fireplace.

"Our biggest problem was financial. Our contracts were down mostly because of the economy, and we've had to lay a few people off, but I really don't think there's any connection."

"Any other problems, Mr. Upstein?" Steve asked.

Upstein paused in thought. "Mostly financial, but Bill Chenowith could fill you in better than I on that subject."

Doc turned to Gordon. "Who is Chenowith with?"

Gordon checked a small notebook.

"Sergeant Wilson and Bob Zimmerman, in Porter Hall."

"Get them over here!"

Sergeant Allen Wilson was from District Thirty-Three of the Indiana State Police out of Bloomington, Indiana. His investigative team normally would pursue drug violations, but because of the apparent urgency of the situation, his group was called in. Sergeant Allen, an African American, was extremely soft spoken, which belied his muscular six-foot-two frame. He had been with the state police for fifteen years and had developed a reputation for investigative prowess. Sergeant Wilson, along with Zimmerman, sat beside Bill Chenowith and gestured toward Doc and Steve.

"Tell them what you told us earlier."

Chenowith, noticeably irritated, took a deep breath.

"Pence was in the process of trying to sell the company," Chenowith said slowly.

"Sell the company?" Upstein bolted up-right.

"You didn't know this?" Doc responded.

"Good God!" Upstein screamed. "Executive vice president of the company, and he didn't have enough confidence in me to tell me?"

Chenowith gave Upstein a bewildered look.

Sergeant Wilson intervened.

"All right, all right, let's calm down. Tell them the rest."

Chenowith rubbed his chin, nervously looking at Dan Upstein.

"He wanted me to make adjustments in the books."

"What do you mean 'adjustments'?" Allen asked.

"We were going busted. He wanted me to make some changes to make our net worth look better," Chenowith answered.

"What kind of changes?" Doc questioned.

"Nothing that others haven't done to make things look better. It's called reversing write-downs," Chenowith responded.

"That legal?" Doc continued.

"It's not illegal, but it's unethical as hell if you don't disclose it to the buyers."

"Did Pence intend to disclose it to them?" Steve asked.

"That's beside the point!" Upstein interrupted. "Why wasn't I informed about all this?"

Sergeant Wilson ignored the question.

"Pence never told me what he intended to reveal to potential buyers," Chenowith answered, "but I would imagine he would have."

Upstein leaned his forearms on his knees and hung his head in disgust. There was a moment of silence as Wilson wrote in his notebook.

"Okay, let's go in another direction. I understand that Pence had been drinking heavily last night. Is that right?"

The sergeant looked at Upstein.

"We had our own bottles. We started drinking about four forty-five last night in my room, and it seemed to be hitting Gerald pretty hard. I suggested we go to the lodge restaurant about six thirty, but he said he wasn't hungry. I left him in my room and went to join the others in the restaurant."

Steve chimed in. "What time did he go back to his room?"

"I came back to my room about eight o'clock. He was still there. We talked and drank some more, and then I took him to his room around midnight," Upstein responded.

"And in all this time he never mentioned selling the company?" Steve inquired.

"Never."

Chenowith jumped up, walked to the fireplace then glared fiercely at Upstein. Steve noticed, wondered what it meant, but shrugged it off and continued his questioning.

"Out of curiosity," Steve said, "what the hell did you talk about?"

"His experimental aircraft," Upstein answered.

Glances were exchanged.

"His what?"

Upstein half smiled and shook his head. "Gerald may not have been much of an administrator, but he was a genius in developing complicated computer programs. The XSA, as he coded it, was a dream of his. An aircraft that is totally computer operated. The concept is not new, but his idea raises it to an incredible new level. I'm not sure he would have shown me it all if he hadn't been three sheets to the wind."

Steve was intrigued.

"Showed you?"

"Yes, he had drawings with him . . . in his brief case."

"What briefcase? We didn't find a briefcase in his room." Doc glanced at Steve for confirmation.

"My God, that's right," Chenowith shot back.

"He had it with him yesterday, but it wasn't in his room this morning."

Wilson went back to his notebook.

"So-o-o, we have one missing CEO and the plans for one missing X . . ."

"XSA," Upstein said.

"Whatever."

It was getting dark, but there would be enough light yet to give Steve Gordon visibility for a quick tour of the park area. Snow had been falling for the last two hours, and over three inches was already on the ground. The remainder of the team was back at the lodge going over the day's interviews, and the Pence group had been sent back to their rooms where they were to stay until further notice. Steve had dismissed himself to make one last patrol of the area before dark.

The two missing hunters could have innocently left the park through one of the two other exits, but that was against the established rules of the deer hunt, and in his gut, Steve believed they were still somewhere inside the park. If so, what were they up to? Were they, as Steve suspected, linked to the missing Gerry Pence?

He drove south passed the park office and turned left toward Sharon Campground. The roads were snow covered and treacherous. The descent down the steep winding road was a challenge, so Steve's mind for the moment was on maneuvering the van. At the bottom, the road leveled off, and his thoughts then went back to the early hours of the day and the questioning of the Pence group.

Sergeant Wilson's state police forensic team had screened all five of the group's rooms but, aside from the bullet hole in the window and the blood stains on the floor in Gerald Pence's room, the others had been clean. Then there were the drops of blood leading out of the room, down the hallway toward the west exit. They were small drops, and the way they were spaced led the team to conclude that, if indeed it was a gunshot wound, it was not serious. The drops led to the parking lot and stopped, leading to the theory that the victim had been placed in a vehicle.

Then there was the phone number found in the cell phone in Pence's room. Jason Bonneau had tried the number. Pence's daughter, Becky, had answered and told Bonneau that her mother was out of town—supposedly in Chicago. Jason told the girl that it was very important that we get in touch with her as soon as possible, but elected not to tell her why.

It continued to snow, and the evening light was fading. Steve approached the Sharon shelter. He suddenly pumped the brakes. There was movement behind the shelter. Was it a deer? He pulled the van to the side of the road and peered into the haze of falling snow. It was no deer. There was a dark figure moving through the trees away from him. He opened the window and shouted.

"You! What are you doing there?"

The figure disappeared into the woods. Steve rang up Doc Ewing on the truck radio.

"Doc, we've got some activity here. I'm down by the Sharon Lake shelter. I'm going on foot in pursuit!"

"No, no, Steve, stay where you are! We'll be there in a few minutes!"

Steve never heard Doc. He was out of the van and moving across the field toward the woods. The snow had subsided somewhat, and there was still enough light that Steve could see footprints leading into the thicket. He followed cautiously. The footprints led up the hill, but as he moved deeper into the woods, the trees began filtering out the light and the prints became obscure. Suddenly, he froze.

Steve focused his eyes on a dark form standing halfway up the hill.

He moved toward it slowly.

"Identify yourself!" he shouted.

There was no response, but Steve would never have heard it anyway. A sharp blow struck him from the rear. All went black, and he crumbled to the ground.

Steve was aware of the flashing red light reflecting on the snow and the trees around him. Casey Roger's face came into focus and beyond him, standing, was Doc.

"Some guys just have to be the hero! Why the hell didn't you stay put like I told you?"

Rubbing his throbbing head, Steve looked up. "I didn't hear you," he said haltingly. "What's happening?"

"Can you get up?" Casey asked.

"I think so." Steve extended his hand, and the two men pulled him to his feet.

"Wow. What hit me?" He massaged the back of his head. No blood—just a large bump.

"Whoever belted you took off over the hill when he saw us coming. Deputy Bentley and Bob Zimmerman are tracking him," Casey said.

"He's probably armed, Casey. I think I got the butt end of a pistol."

"I'm calling in some back-up," said Casey as he took Steve by the arm. "Let's get you back to the van."

Sergeant Wilson responded to Casey's call.

"I've got some troopers on the way, Sheriff. I wouldn't get too aggressive until we get there."

"Bentley and Zimmerman are trailing our fugitive. We think we've found at least one of our lost hunters," Casey reported.

"I repeat, hold up pursuit until my men arrive!"

Two shots rang out from over the hill.

"Too late, Sergeant! We've got problems here. Hurry the hell up!"

Three more shots followed.

"Hell, there's a fire fight going on up there. We're going in, Sergeant. We'll see you when we see you!"

Casey grabbed a shotgun from the rack in the back seat of his car and tossed it to Doc. Pulling his service pistol, he turned to Steve.

"You stay here, Steve. You're in no shape for this."

"The hell you say!" Steve shot back as he jumped from his van.

The three men moved into the woods and up the hill. Near the crest they came across Bob Zimmerman propped against a tree, bleeding heavily from the shoulder. He was barely conscious. In his hand was Ted Bently's service pistol.

"Where's Ted?" Casey asked as he kneeled beside the fallen park manager. Bob struggled out a response.

"He took two hits. I grabbed his gun and fired back before they got me. I think I hit one of them."

He began losing consciousness. Casey shook him back.

"Two? There were two of them?"

"Y-y-yes . . . get up there. I think Ted's in bad shape."

Casey took the pistol from Zimmerman and handed it to Steve.

"There's a first aid kit in the trunk of my car, Steve. Get this guy patched up as best you can. We're going on up. When they get here, tell the sergeant we could use some help."

They moved out, and Steve helped the crippled Zimmerman back to the sheriff's squad car. It took Sergeant Wilson and another state police car as back-up just fifteen minutes to arrive. He paged Casey on his cell phone.

"This is Wilson, Rogers. What's going on?"

A short delay followed.

"We need an ambulance up here. Bentley is alive, but barely. We're up in the CCC shelter. We also found a trail of blood leading to some tire tracks that led away toward the south gate. Maybe we can still cut them off!"

Wilson frantically motioned to the driver in the other car.

"Get to the south gate and see if you can intercept them! Go, go!"

The car squirreled off in the snow toward the gate. Wilson turned to Steve who was winding up his first aid on Zimmerman.

"We need an ambulance here, Steve. I'll drive up the road toward the shelter. Maybe we'll get lucky and run into whoever they are."

He was gone. Zimmerman grabbed Steve's arm.

"During the exchange of fire up there, one of them shouted something to the other. Steve . . . I could swear it sounded like a woman!"

CHAPTER 3

Two full-time female clerks had been given permission to finish decorating the large tree centered below the cathedral ceiling in the lobby of the lodge. Boxes that had contained the garlands and bulbs lay scattered about as they stood on high ladders, heightening the Christmas spirit as best they could.

Two people entered through the front door and wound their way through the maze of boxes to the front desk. One carried a large television camera on his shoulder, the other, a woman, wore a maroon jacket bearing the inscription WITV, CH 14. The woman addressed the desk clerk.

"I'm here to see a Stephen Gordon."

The clerk responded nervously, "I . . . I'm not sure he's available right now."

He looked up toward the balcony above. Steve stood at the railing looking down at the group.

"That's okay, I'll talk to them." He motioned to the two. "Come on up."

"I hope you don't mind us taping this interview, Mr. Gordon," asked the young women as they sat in the settee by the fireplace.

"No, no. Go ahead."

Steve sat in the stuffed chair across from them.

"Mr. Gordon, how long has this Mr. Pence been missing?" she asked, moving her microphone toward him.

"This will be the third day."

"And the park has been closed to the public for that length of time?" she asked, motioning to the cameraman to continue shooting.

"Yes, and it will stay closed until we resolve this thing."

"I also understand that the situation has evolved into a criminal issue and that two of your men have been shot by unknown assailants."

Steve wove his fingers together between his knees and shifted nervously. "Yes-yes, that's the situation."

"Any idea what this is all about?" she asked.

"Ma'am, you seem to know as much as we do at this point."

"What is the condition of the two who were shot?"

"Zimmerman had a shoulder wound and is fine. Ted Bentley is more serious and is in the hospital in Bloomington, but it looks like he'll pull through," Steve answered.

"That's good news, Mr. Gordon. Do you have any idea who did the shooting?"

"Not the slightest."

"I understand that they escaped out of the park after the altercation. Any idea where they might have gone?"

Steve was getting impatient. "They apparently got through the south exit. There was too much traffic on 135 and with all the snow we couldn't tell whose tracks were whose."

"And what about the FBI?"

Steve looked surprised. "What about the FBI?"

An awkward pause as she studied his expression.

"You didn't know that the FBI has been called into this?"

Steve rose quickly and motioned for the camera and microphone to be cut. "No I didn't, and until I find out as much about this as you guys apparently do, this interview is over!"

The young woman's face flushed as she stood up. "I hope I haven't offended you, Mr. Gordon. I . . . I just thought . . ."

Steve took the interviewer and the cameraman by the arms and ushered them toward the steps.

"That's okay, just no more interviews for the time being."

The two moved back through the boxes in the lobby and toward the door. The woman looked up at Steve as he stood by the railing.

"I'm sorry, Mr. Gordon."

Steve pulled out his pager and pushed Doc Ewing's number. It rang twice and Doc came on.

"What is it, Steve?"

"Doc, do you know something you haven't told me."

"What are you talking about?"

"Are you at the office?"

"Yeah!"

"I'll be right there."

Steve and Doc sat in the park office listening to Sergeant Wilson on the "squawk box."

"I was going to call you guys this morning about this. It seems that someone in the governor's office called in a local FBI special agent about the situation here and the media got a hold of it."

"But why the FBI?" Doc asked.

"This whole thing smacks of an abduction, and that's right up the FBI's alley. But listen to this! An FBI special agent out of Chicago has been in touch with the Indianapolis branch regarding the missing president of Porter Aviation Company, headquartered in Chicago."

Doc shouted into the CB, "Aviation? Would that tie in with Pence's project?"

There was a pause as if Wilson was reviewing some notes.

"You mean this experimental thing? It could, but how?"

"I don't know, but it might be a good idea to talk to Upstein and Chenowith again."

Steve nodded his approval and spoke up. "They might be able to shed some light on any connection here. I think we should give them all another review." Steve added, "Maybe something will come out that didn't before."

There was another pause.

"You might be right, but remember, these people have families and we can't hold them forever," Wilson retorted.

"Okay! Let's get them together this morning, and if you're satisfied with the results, we'll send them all home. I'll see you in the lodge in one hour," Doc said. He hung up and shook his head.

"What next, Steve? We're on the front page of at least a half dozen big city papers. Our little state park has earned feature story status in most all local and network radio and television stations and now with the FBI."

Steve chuckled sardonically. "Whatever happened to our simple little deer hunt?"

Agent Chuck Manning worked out of the Chicago FBI office. He had recently been put on what he thought was a routine missing persons case until it turned into a possible kidnapping. There was apparently some connection with a case out of Indianapolis via Williams Creek, Indiana, and the Williams Creek State Park. He now sat in the office of Indianapolis Agent Kyle Broyles.

"This guy Daryl Atkins is the CEO of Porter Aviation." Manning asserted as he lounged in the stuffed chair in front of Broyles's desk and stared at the document in his hand.

"He disappeared three days ago." He continued. "When we investigated, we found out that he and his company had been doing some high stakes business with Pence Technology here in Indy."

Broyles leaned forward shoving another paper toward Manning and said, "When I reported the Gerald Pence connection with Porter, you put two and two together . . . so we've got ourselves an interstate situation."

Broyles rose and strolled to the window of his office overlooking north Pennsylvania Street. The holiday season was conspicuous on store fronts across from their building. The morning rush hour was just winding down and traffic, despite piles of plowed snow on either side of the avenue, was running smoothly.

He turned to Manning. "Mind if I smoke?" he asked, pulling a pack of Marlboros from his pocket.

"I'd rather you didn't, but what the hell—it's your place." Manning smiled.

Agent Broyles shrugged and placed the pack back into his pocket. He returned to his desk, opened a drawer and withdrew a pack of gum. He offered a stick to his visitor, was waved off, and stuck one into his mouth.

"In lieu of smoking." He chuckled.

Broyles sat and stared at the open file in front of him. He massaged his temples absently. "According to the state police investigative unit down there, Pence had kept this sale under wraps from most of his execs. Only this Chenowith guy, their CFO, was in on it."

He flipped to another page in the file. "According to the record there was a little creative accounting to make things look better to the buyer."

"How many in Pence's company knew about that?" asked Manning.

"Only Pence and Chenowith as far as we know. I imagine we had some pretty pissed off execs when the truth came out." Manning grinned.

"Their executive VP seemed to be rather upset!"

"Enough to react violently?"

"I don't think so. Apparently, he didn't know about the sale plans until afterward. Although, to tell the truth, no one in that group had a real alibi for their whereabouts during that time of the night . . . or morning."

"So any one of them could have . . ."

"Naw!" Broyles said. "I doubt it. They were all accounted for during that fire fight."

He closed the file folder and leaned back, "No, everything points to outside involvement. They think two hunters who were unaccounted for when they closed down the deer hunt had something to do with all this. They think they were the ones who did the shooting."

"What about this project that Pence was supposed to be working on?" Manning asked.

"The X . . . whatever? It's an experimental aircraft that's supposed to do everything including your laundry."

Broyles reopened the file folder and sifted through several pages before pulling one out. He studied it momentarily.

"He calls it the XSA. Don't ask me what that stands for. It's supposed to be the cutting edge of aircraft technology. That's all we know. But the guys down there report that a brief case containing some details of the craft is missing."

Manning stood up and stretched. "And you think this might be behind all this."

"An aircraft production company trying to buy out a computer chip manufacturing firm? Missing CEOs of both companies and missing experimental aircraft designs? If it isn't related, it's one hell of a coincidence!"

Manning pulled a small pad from his coat pocket and flipped through it. He stopped at a page and looked up. "You haven't mentioned Pence's wife. What's her status?"

Broyles sat back and shook his head. "Now that's another story. Her daughter says she went up your way three days ago and hasn't returned."

Manning ran his fingers through his hair and grinned. "So do we have another missing person?"

"She was supposed to be back home yesterday according to her daughter, and when she didn't show up, the daughter called the police," Broils responded.

Manning returned the pad to his pocket and walked to the window.

"Well, well, well . . ." He turned toward Broyles. "The wife of the missing Indianapolis CEO runs off to Chicago, where another missing CEO, linked to the first missing CEO, and winds up missing herself. What does that say to you?" he asked.

Broils removed his gum and wadded it up in its wrapper. "If that doesn't tie into this whole thing, then we have another one hell of a coincidence."

CHAPTER 4

With exception of CFO Bill Chenowith and Janet Taylor, Pence's secretary, the rest of the corporate group was released to return to Indianapolis under the provision that they would be accessible for further questioning.

Bill and Janet sat at the conference table in Cagle Hall with Steve Gordon and Sergeant Allen Wilson. Doc Ewing had received word that two FBI agents were on their way to the park to review the situation, so he had asked Steve to take his place.

Chenowith was visibly irritated.

"Sergeant, Janet is quite distraught over all this. There's nothing she can tell you that I can't."

"No, no . . . I'm all right, Bill. Maybe there are some things they should know."

Chenowith glared at the secretary.

"Janet!" he squirmed, his face reddening.

Steve leaned toward Wilson and spoke in an audible whisper.

"Let me talk to her privately, Allen."

At the sergeant's nod, Steve rose and motioned Janet Taylor to follow him. Chenowith jumped to his feet and darted toward the two.

"This is an outrage!" he screamed. "I won't allow this. What she has to say, she can say in front of us all!"

"Cool it, man."

Chenowith reluctantly obeyed as he watched the two leave the meeting room.

He stared nervously toward the door as the sergeant continued his interrogation.

"You seem to be concerned about what Ms. Taylor might say. Why?"

Chenowith squirmed nervously.

"Janet is very close to Pence. She's his confidant, in fact. She and I, as far as I know, are the only ones who know about Pence and his wife."

Wilson looked up from his note pad.

"His wife?"

"Let me digress. Upstein says he doesn't think Pence's disappearance has anything to do with the sale of Pence Technology. I know it has everything to do with it! The head of Porter Aviation in Chi—"

Wilson interrupted. "A Daryl Atkins."

Chenowith was startled.

"Yes . . . yes, how did you . . ."

"He's been reported missing, and Pence's wife has also disappeared—both within the same time frame."

"Okay . . . that figures," Chenowith responded with conviction.

He rose and moved to the fireplace. He turned to the sergeant.

"Listen to this: Atkins and Darlene Pence were having an affair. Gerald didn't find out about it until about two months ago."

Chenowith returned to his seat and leaned toward Wilson.

"It all apparently started with the trips they were taking to Chicago to talk to this Atkins guy about the buyout. I guess Darlene and he hit it off and began seeing each other under one pretense or another, mostly related to Porter's alleged interest in purchasing Pence Technology."

Wilson wrote in his notebook and then looked up.

"What do you mean, 'alleged'?"

"I don't think Atkins or Porter was really interested in our company at all. They, and particularly Atkins, were interested in Gerald's project."

"The . . . the . . . ," Wilson stuttered, flipping through his book.

"The XSA. It's my feeling that Atkins was using his relationship with Pence's wife to get to the XSA!"

Wilson rubbed the back of his neck. He was confused.

"How does this all relate to Janet Taylor?"

"It's been obvious for quite some time—to me at least— that Janet has had a more than passive feeling for Gerald Pence. Pence couldn't cover his hurt over the situation at home, and Janet made it clear that she was there to console him. It wasn't long before Gerald began leaning on her and naturally one thing lead to another."

Wilson shook his head.

"Don't tell me!"

"It's not what you think. With those two it's all clean, but there's definitely an attachment."

"Okay, Chenowith . . . again, how does this all fit in?"

Chenowith rose and walked to the window. He stood silently for a moment, watched a new snow shower fall lightly on the lawn and road outside, and then turned to Wilson.

"Pence confided to Janet that he had no intention of linking the plans to his XSA to the sale of the corporation. If and when Porter Aviation bought us out, Pence planned to retire and take the aircraft project with him."

The Sergeant was silent for a moment as he wrote in his notebook. He looked up. "Did Atkins know this?"

"Janet told me that Pence told her of a horrendous confrontation he had with his wife over her affair with Atkins. It was then that he told her that he would never include the XSA plans with the sale of the company. You can be sure that that bit of news went straight to Mr. Lover."

At that moment Steve and Janet reentered the meeting room. Steve motioned toward a chair at the table and Janet sat down. He turned to Wilson and Chenowith.

"Mr. Chenowith, if you've told Sergeant Wilson what Ms. Taylor here has told me, then I think we have several interesting possibilities."

He turned his attention to Wilson.

"Remember what I told you Zimmerman said during that gun fight the other evening?"

Steve didn't wait for an answer.

"He said that he thought one of the assailants sounded like a woman."

Chenowith walked from the window.

"Are you suggesting that . . . that . . ." Wilson finished the thought, saying, "That the woman could have been Darlene Pence?!"

CHAPTER 5

Doc Ewing and Sheriff Casey Roberts had just finished the tour of the area with Agents Manning and Broyles and were piling into the park office. Doc prepared a fresh pot of coffee and distributed filled foam cups to the two FBI agents. He made a toasting gesture and sat behind his desk. He motioned for the others to sit.

The agents had flown in by helicopter from Indianapolis after calling ahead to confirm the availability of an authority to talk to. The 'copter had landed in the open field directly across from the park office. Doc had stood by the fence bordering the field, observing the copter's descent. The swish-swish-swish sound had brought back old memories—a field just like this in Vietnam.

His mind wandered.

The sound of gun fire could be heard even over the swish-swish-swish of the Huey. Marines were loading the wounded and dead bodies onto his 'copter as the battle raged intensely around him. He was choking on the smoke and acrid smell of nitrate. A marine captain shouted through the cockpit window.

"We're takin' a pastin', Lieutenant.

We gotta get out of here now. We need more 'copters?!"

Doc hung his head out the port.

"It's nearly dark, Captain. I don't know if it's possible, but I'll sure as hell try!"

He lifted his helicopter off and swung over the burning fields and forest toward the rear and the Plei Me Special Forces camp. He'd been fired on over the Ia Tae River but managed to make it back to his base with no extensive damage. After unloading his human cargo, he delivered the marine captain's plea for relief.

"We've only got three Hueys available Lieutenant, and it's almost dark. Those guys are going to have to dig in and hold 'til morning."

"Colonel, if you add my 'copter, it makes four, and we can get 'em all out with one run," Doc shouted.

"Hell, Lieutenant, you're in no condition to go back there. It's suicide!"

"Those marines are taking a pasting back there, Colonel, and I intend to help as many of them as I can."

Doc pushed his helmet onto his head and backed off toward the refueled Huey. "Okay, okay, Lieutenant! But at least wait until the others are ready to go."

Within fifteen minutes the four helicopters were airborne and heading to the battle zone. By this time the sun had sunk below the mountain ridges and the twilight began to make visibility difficult. Across the Ia Tae River and then the La Meur and then the glow of the fire fight below. The 'copters descended into the swirl of smoke and what was left of the marine unit dashed across the open field toward them. There were screams of commands as the warriors scrambled aboard the Hueys. The din was deafening but miraculously all four craft lifted off with their loads and headed back to safety. It was not until his return to the SF camp that Doc realized that he had been grazed in the arm by a stray bullet.

"Well, Lieutenant," the colonel said, grinning, "it looks like you hit pay dirt. Not only will you get the Purple Heart for that scratch, but I'm recommending you for the Silver Star!"

The swishing stopped and Doc had returned to the present and the voice of one of the FBI Agents.

"I'm special agent Kyle Broyles from the Indianapolis FBI Office." He gestured toward his companion. "And this is Agent Chuck Manning from the Chicago office."

The four of them shook hands, and the tour of the site begun. After several hours, they ended up in Doc's office.

"We are winding up the third day since this all started, gentlemen, and we don't know a whole lot more than we did then," Doc said after his first sip of coffee.

Agent Manning leaned back in his chair to pick up his attaché case beside him on the floor. He placed it on his lap and opened it. "The way this is all developing, I think the thing has a lot more to it than the disappearance of one man." He pulled out a document and slipped it across the desk toward Doc. He continued. "How about the disappearance of three people—all tied in to each other."

Doc glanced passively at the paper in front of him and took another sip of his coffee. "We were aware of all this, but to my knowledge, had not drawn any conclusions. What do you guys think?"

Manning pointed to the paper. Doc studied the sheet in front of him more closely, while the two agents remained silent. Moments later, he looked up with an expression of amazement on his face.

"Are you sure of this?" He inquired.

"We interviewed Darlene Pence's daughter at the Pence's home, and on the basis of what she told us, we checked the passenger list at the American Airlines desk."

"They were on it?" Doc returned.

"Both of them! Daryl Atkins and Darlene Pence flew to the Cayman Islands three days ago."

"Then the high pitched voice . . ."

"Couldn't have been Darlene Pence," Agent Manning said.

They sat at a table in front of a series of French windows in the Cafe Havana in the Westin Casuarina Hotel. Through the windows, the Caribbean embraced the golden shimmer of the setting sun. Darlene and Daryl arrived at the Grand Cayman Island that afternoon, went directly to the hotel, and checked in as man and wife under an assumed name. No sooner had they settled in their suite, than Darlene began drinking. In disgust, Daryl cut it short and suggested that they eat an early dinner and then tour the island. Darlene had resisted but complied, with the understanding that she could order drinks at the restaurant.

She had ordered a vodka martini, downed it and ordered another. Daryl took her hand and forced a smile.

"Hey, Mrs. 'Barry', don't leave me now. We've got a lot to do in the next couple of days!"

"Like what?!" She slurred.

Just two years ago, Darlene was considered a beauty. Her five-foot-nine-inch frame would have made any professional model envious. Distinct facial features—well sculptured and balanced—were enhanced by a slight in-turn of the left eye, which gave the impression that she was looking straight through whoever she was with. Her soft blonde hair had flowed gently to her shoulders, framing a long, graceful neck.

Daryl remembered all this from a large oil portrait of her that hung above the fireplace mantel in the great room of her Indianapolis home. She was now aging far beyond her years. Her hair was scraggly, face swollen, large bags sat under bloodshot eyes, and mouth drooped in perpetual bitterness. It was such a shame, Daryl thought.

He reached across the table and took her hand again.

"Let's get something in our stomach and then go for a little stroll up the coast."

She blanched at the suggestion and pulled away.

"Tomorrow," he said, "after I attend to some personal business, we can do a little scuba diving."

Her second martini arrived. She ate the olive and took a long pull on the drink. She put the half-empty glass down and stared defiantly at Daryl.

"I haven't gone scuba diving for years . . . and what personal business could you possibly have down here?"

"A little banking. It shouldn't take long. Then we can . . ."

She cut him short. "What kind of banking?"

He was becoming irritated. "You wouldn't be interested."

"The hell I wouldn't! In fact, why don't I go with you in the morning, and then we can go diving."

Daryl's patience played out. "Dammit. No, Darlene! It has nothing to do with you."

She drained her glass and motioned for the waiter. She leaned toward Daryl. "It was your idea for me to come to the Cayman Islands with you. Against my better judgment I went along with it. I've burned all my bridges now, pal, so everything you do from here on out has everything to do with me!"

"Let me remind you, my dear," Daryl shot back, "I took one hell of a risk bringing you. If Upstein should find out . . . !"

Darlene laughed. "Screw, Upstein!"

Daryl waved the waiter off and stood up. "You've had your last drink for the night, Darlene. Let's get out of here. Maybe in the morning when you've sobered up, you'll be a little more reasonable."

Darlene's sour mood was not much better the next morning. Her head throbbed almost to the point of nausea as she squinted at Daryl as he dressed.

"Refresh my memory. Where the hell are you going?" Her voice crackled through parched lips.

Daryl stood in front of the full-length mirror on the wall opposite the queen sized bed, putting the final touches to his tie.

He assessed his appearance. He was shorter than Darlene at five-foot-eight inches, and even with lifter heels he couldn't achieve eye-level height. That bothered him.

Another thing bothered him was that his head was out of proportion to his slight body, exaggerated by a full head of black hair. But he was muscular, in good health, and by most standards, handsome. He was satisfied with that.

He glanced at Darlene through the mirror.

"After last night, it wouldn't surprise me if you couldn't remember where you were."

She rose to one elbow, and to be sure Daryl wasn't right, she looked out the sliding glass door toward the Caribbean surf for reassurance. She dropped back.

"Wise ass!" She cupped her hand over her eyes and moaned in pain. "I need a drink."

"If you can't remember where I'm going, then you wouldn't remember what happened last night."

She again rose to her elbow. "What happened last night?" She looked about the room and then back to Daryl. She rubbed her forehead and then brightened.

"Wait a minute . . . last night. Hell, we had a fight."

Daryl walked over to the desk by the glass door and retrieved his wallet and watch. "About what? Do you remember?" He slipped his watch on and came over to the bed.

"I wasn't as drunk as you thought, Atkins. It's all coming back to me. You have a suitcase full of money. I remember that."

He glared down at her. "You had no business nosing into that. What else did we talk about?"

She waved him off. "I'll have to think about that, but if I remember, you wouldn't tell me how much money was there or where you got it."

"Because it isn't any of your damn business!" he barked.

He walked to the shelf in the closet and pulled down a large attaché case. Darlene swung to the edge of the bed and gestured toward him.

"Bastard! You got me now, and for better or worse. What's mine is yours, and . . . by God . . . what's yours is mine!"

Daryl rushed to the top dresser drawer, opened it and pulled out a half-empty bottle of vodka. He slammed it on the desk beside her.

"Here, you bitch! You do need a drink. Be dressed and ready to go when I get back."

He went to the door, attaché case in hand, opened it and turned.

"And don't be too drunk . . . booze and scuba diving don't mix."

He walked out and slammed the door behind him.

Daryl drove the rental minvan from the hotel south on West Bay Road toward George Town. He was scheduled at Barclays Bank at nine thirty, so he could drive at his leisure.

Darlene Pence's actions of late had upset him. Her sudden possessiveness, her lack of cooperation, and, of course, her heavy drinking were disconcerting. Daryl wasn't sure how much she really knew about the money in the attaché case, or what his plans were for it. If she had any idea, God knows what she would do.

West Bay became North Church Street as he entered the city. Still plenty of time.

What bothered him the most about her was her refusal to do anything further to assist him in gaining access to her husband's, as she put it, "stupid toy!" That's part of what they had argued about last evening. The XSA was at the center of all this, and she wasn't going to follow through with her end of the bargain.

North Church became Harbour Drive. He was only minutes away from the bank.

No, he thought, Darlene Pence had changed and was of no further use to him.

He stood at the dock at Spanish Bay at the northern tip of the Grand Cayman watching the approach of a small yacht. As it grew in size, Daryl's thoughts went back to the events of the day. He had deposited $350,000 at Barclays Bank as an offshore asset protection trust under the name of Harold Hopkins. This had been the third deposit in a two-year period and had brought the total in the account under that name to over $2.75 million. This, as with the other deposits, would find its way safely to a bank in Switzerland.

The boat's engines subsided as it began to turn its stern toward the dock. They roared to life temporarily and began a glide backward toward Daryl and the dock. It came aside, and a voice boomed through a megaphone.

"Hop aboard, Mr. Atkins, and we'll get the hell out of here."

Daryl hopped onto the deck and nearly lost his balance as the yacht lurched forward in full power. A burly, slovenly character swung down from the flying bridge and approached him. He extended a huge hand.

"I'm Jack Lynch, the skipper of this tub." He looked around inquisitively and then back to Atkins.

"You alone?" Lynch asked.

"Yes, yes, I'm alone."

"I thought . . ."

Daryl clutched Lynch's arm and walked unsteadily with him toward the steps leading below.

"You thought wrong. My companion has decided to stay in the Caymans for a while. How long until the rendezvous?"

The skipper glanced skyward. "If he's on schedule, we should pick him up in about a half hour."

Daryl nodded and went below. He was offered and accepted a beer from the galley. He sat at the table by a porthole and stared out at the spray of sea beating up against the glass. The beer bottle was opened and he took a long swallow. The roll of the boat drifted him back to earlier in the day.

When he had returned to the hotel, Darlene was dressed and ready to go. Although she had been drinking, she was in an amazingly good mood. She was eager to go, so they boarded the minvan and drove north to an offbeat dive operator by the name of Diago's Dive. Although normally a certification card was required to obtain scuba equipment, Daryl's generous monetary offering procured all that was needed. He told the clerk that they were both quite experienced and needn't be accompanied by an instructor.

They then drove to a dive site further north at West Bay. Donning their gear, Daryl had suggested they try the shallow off-shore waters to avoid the necessity of hiring a boat. He followed Darlene into the water, submerging finally into the wonderworld of coral and sponges. After a short distance and deeper water, Daryl swam next to Darlene, reached for her mask, and yanked it from her face. She turned and fought him. Her fingernails dug into his chest as he pushed her deeper. No, Darlene my dear, he thought, you are no longer of any use to me.

Her struggles stopped, and she slid underneath him into the depths below.

The skipper's voice aroused him from his reverie.

"She's here, Mr. Atkins. Right on schedule!"

He went above and watched as a Cessna 206 seaplane splashed down to their starboard. The yacht cut its engines and drifted slowly to a stop as the aircraft approached. Alongside, Daryl boarded and gave a thumbs-up to Skipper Lynch as the plane pulled away and gunned across the water into the evening sky.

CHAPTER 6

Steve's office was located in the park nature center. It was off the main exhibit area, small and cluttered, but it was quiet and his sanctuary, especially during the winter off-season. Outside the office door to the far left was the auditorium where nature presentations were given to tourists during the busy season. To the immediate left was the hallway leading to the bird-watching room. This was one of Steve's favorite retreats, and there he sat on the wooden bench, staring through the one-way window at the assortment of birds clustered around the feeders outside the center. Their chirping was magnified through the internal speaker system. Watching birds to him was like staring mindlessly into a crackling fire in a fireplace—it was therapeutic.

This was the time of year when the bird activity peaked, and as Steve sat there, he thought it was too bad that there were so few people to enjoy them. His mind temporarily wandered from the problems of the past several days back to the day at home when he had installed a similar feeding station, complete with a one-way window and sound system. The boys, then nine and ten years of age, were thrilled and had invited neighborhood friends to meet the thrills of nature and their ingenious dad.

That was eleven years ago. Steven Jr. was now twenty-one years old and was in his junior year at Indiana University. Bobby was twenty and was finishing up his sophomore year at Purdue. Considering the many arguments between the two siblings, Steve often wondered if sending them to rival schools was such a good idea, but since the boys were following in their father's footsteps with a major of forestry, they had more in common than not and got along as well as could be expected.

His thoughts turned to his wife, Carolyn. A recent mammogram had revealed a small lump in her left breast, and she was due for a lumpectomy after the holidays. Hopefully, they had caught it in time, and it would not be considered serious, but it had given them a scare. Steve could not imagine life without Carolyn.

Steve rose and strolled back toward his office. Strains of "Oh Little Town of Bethlehem" drifted from a small radio on the bookshelf beside his desk. He sat and absently listened to the music. He then looked down at the notes he had written earlier. They sketched the series of events occurring since this past Friday morning. Did anything make sense? Could any of the questions they provoked be answered? Was the missing Pence still in the park? Over a dozen people had scoured the area to no avail! Was he still alive? There was no way of knowing, but Steve's gut feeling said he was. Who and where were the two missing hunters? It seemed at first that they might be none other than Pence's wife and her lover, Daryl Atkins, but the shocking news that the two had departed for the Caymans before Pence's disappearance seemed to eliminate that possibility. Who then was the woman Zimmerman thought he heard during the shootout Friday evening? What about the company executives, who by now were all home in Indianapolis? Steve leaned back in his chair. This point bothered him. How is it possible for an Executive Vice president to be so far out of the loop that he had no knowledge that the president and CEO of the company was in negotiations to sell out? How, in fact, could the others not have some idea—by rumor if nothing else? No, there was something missing here. As good at his job as Sergeant Wilson was and in spite of the expertise of the two FBI agents, there were some questions that had not been asked.

"God Bless Yea Merry Gentlemen" drifted from the radio as Steve picked up the phone and dialed Doc Ewing's office. It rang twice and Doc's voice came on.

"Ewing here."

"Doc, this is Steve. I've got a special favor to ask of you. With all the help we have down here now, I'd like a couple of days off."

"Steve, you're my PR guy! Who'll talk to the media when they hit us again?"

"I want to go to Indianapolis, Doc, and I can kill two birds with one stone."

"How's that?

"Carolyn wants to go Christmas shopping up there, and while she's at it, I can hit several TV and radio stations and the newspaper. That'll get them off our backs."

There was a pause as Doc processed the idea. "Okay," he reluctantly replied, "but keep me posted and be back here by Wednesday. And, Steve . . . no funny stuff."

Steve placed the phone back on the receiver and smiled. Yes, sir, he thought. No funny stuff.

Steve left Carolyn in their room at the Hyatt Hotel in Indianapolis with the understanding that she would do her Christmas shopping at the Circle City Mall down the street, while he went about his chores. He had called a brief press conference at the Hyatt involving several television and radio stations and the one major city newspaper. There was not much he could say about the situation. Nothing more had developed in the case, so after a short question-and-answer session, he was on his way to his first stop—Gerald Pence's home—to have a conversation with his daughter, Becky. The house was located north of the city about twenty-five minutes away. After leaving Carolyn to her shopping, he had called Becky and arranged the meeting.

He pulled into a long driveway leading up to a split-level, brick-and-stone structure. It was not pretentious, nor was it large—perhaps slightly over twenty-eight hundred square feet. It sat on a large, wooded lot at a considerable distance from the road.

Steve parked the van by the two-car garage and walked to the front door. It was paneled with two glass sidelights and a transom above. Before he could push the doorbell, he could see a figure approach through the left panel. The door opened.

"Mr. Gordon?" Her young voice was pleasant but confident. "Please come in."

Steve obliged, entering into a high-ceilinged foyer that led to a great room, obviously the main living area.

On the far side were four high windows that allowed in an abundance of natural light and a restful view of the woods behind the house. To his right, above the fireplace mantel, was a life-sized portrait of a beautiful woman. Becky caught his awed expression.

"My mother," she informed softly.

"She is a beautiful woman," Steve said. "You have her eyes and graceful face."

"Thank you," she whispered.

Steve turned his attention to the girl before him. Becky was tall and slim. Her blond hair was done up in a bun around a square, pleasant face. Despite her twenty-eight years, she exuded a great degree of class and maturity. She was not as beautiful as her mother, but she was highly attractive.

She motioned toward one of the overstuffed couches facing the windows.

"Can I get you something to drink, Mr. Gordon?"

Steve shook his head. "No, thank you, Miss Pence." He sat after Becky seated herself across from him.

He took out his notebook and began flipping through it. "I won't be taking up much of your time, Miss Pence."

"Please call me Becky."

"And you call me Steve."

They exchanged smiles.

He stopped at a page in his notebook and looked up. "I don't imagine I have to fill you in on what's happened at this stage of the game."

"No, unfortunately I'm up on the latest, but I'm not sure how much more I can add."

"We found your dad's cell phone in his room at the lodge. It indicated that he had made a call here sometime before his disappearance."

"Yes, he wanted to talk to mother, but she wasn't here."

"What time was that?"

"About seven thirty. I know because Jeopardy was coming on."

"Did he say what it was he wanted to talk to your mother about?"

Becky took a deep breath and paused a moment. "Steve, by now I think you know the situation between my parents."

Steve nodded. "I think Dad was calling just to check on her. He knew that Daryl Atkins was due in town, and that if he was, Mother wouldn't be home." She paused again. This time, it appeared, to fight back tears. "What frightened me was that she left with her suitcase. I tried to reason with her, but she wouldn't listen. I haven't seen her since. I called the police the next morning."

Tears now ran down her cheeks. Steve withered sympathetically.

"Becky, I'm sorry to put you through this. Can you take a few more questions?"

"Yes, yes, Steve. I'm sorry for all this emotion, but it's just that I feel so helpless." She wiped the tears.

"I understand." He waited for Becky to regain her composure before proceeding. "When you talked to your father, could you tell if he had been drinking? Did he sound drunk?"

"No! I've been around him when he's had too much to drink, and he definitely did not sound drunk to me."

Steve studied his notebook thoughtfully and then looked up. "That's strange. Dan Upstein was adamant about his claim that your father was quite drunk on the night of his disappearance."

Becky let out a guffaw. "I'm not sure I'd believe much of anything that man said."

Steve reacted in surprise. "What do you mean?!"

"Dad was not happy with Dan Upstein. Quite frankly, he didn't trust him. He wanted to fire him, but was afraid of the message it would send to the potential buyers."

"Buyers?! There was more than one potential buyer?"

"There were three that I knew of. The one in Chicago, one in Ohio, and one here in Indianapolis. Upstein was against the sale of the company and—"

Steve interrupted. "Upstein claimed he knew nothing of the sale."

"He was lying!"

"This puts a different light on things, Becky. What else can you tell me that might explain your father's disappearance?"

Becky thought for a moment. She rose from the couch and walked to the windows, studying the snow covered scenery outside. Without turning around she said, "If it wasn't so obvious that violence was involved, I'd say Dad was so despondent about Mother that he just took off."

She turned around and moved back to the couch. "But violence was involved, so I can only think that there could be one other reason. His experimental aircraft."

"I'm not an engineer, Becky, and I know avionics has come a long way, but what I'm hearing about this project sounds a little far-fetched."

Becky straightened up in mock indignation. "Not if Gerald R. Pence has anything to do with it! Steve, Dad might raise hell about me doing this, but I want to show you something that not many people have seen."

She rose and motioned for Steve to follow her. They moved to the right of the great room down a hallway. Halfway there she stopped at a service table, opened the top drawer, and withdrew a key. At the end of the hall was a door, which she unlocked and opened.

"This is Dad's studio, where he has done most of his work on the project."

They entered and Steve's jaw dropped as he beheld the room's contents. In the center was a huge drawing table. On the table was page after page of blueprints for what appeared to be the experimental aircraft. But what drew Steve's attention was a model of it on a table in a corner of the room. He approached it cautiously and examined it.

"My God," he whispered in amazement.

The craft was a complete disk . . . or rather a disk within a disk. The inside disk on the topside displayed two vertical stabilizers leading back and over the outside disk. Between the stabilizers and recessed within the space running around the circumference of the top and bottom outside disks were four exhaust ports. The model sat on three tripod landing pads. Toward the rear, close to the ports, was an air intake that ran the width of the lower inside disk. Steve studied the underside of the model craft.

There were two other exhaust ports—one on each side of the outside disk—which indicated to him the capability of vertical take-off and landing. In the center was a scoured outline of a hatch.

Becky stood over him, amused at his childlike awe at what he was looking at. She sensed his desire. "Go ahead, pick it up."

Hesitantly he accepted her invitation. The model was about eighteen inches in diameter and was made of light gray plastic.

"This is a . . . a flying saucer." Steve chuckled.

"Dad calls it 'The Altair' or 'Flying Eagle.'"

He fingered one of the vertical stabilizers and was startled when the inside disk moved. As it did so, the four exhaust ports moved with it.

"That's how it changes direction," Becky said. "As those engine ports turn so does the craft, and it can be done at a high rate of speed."

"Amazing!" Steve said as he placed the model back on the table. He examined the top disk closer. There was no visible canopy. He looked up at Becky.

"How does the pilot see out of this thing?" he asked.

She smiled. "I asked Dad the same thing. He asked me if I'd ever seen the advertisements on the side and windows of city buses and wondered how anyone inside could see out. They can, and although not exactly the same, that's the principle here. But it's strictly for the enjoyment of the pilot and passengers, because the computer does the flying."

Steve shook his head in wonderment. "How far along is this project?"

"I can't tell you that, but I can say that it's a lot further along than anyone thinks."

Steve looked around the room for a moment.

"This project has to cost a bundle. I hope I'm not being too presumptuous in asking, but how is this all being funded?"

"That, Steve, is a long story. I know Dad has legitimate backing, but the who and what I am not privy to."

"What about the government? Wouldn't they be interested in all of this?"

Becky motioned that it was time to vacate the studio. She escorted Steve out into the hallway and locked the door. They walked slowly toward the front door.

"Steve, up until the day before yesterday, the government had no knowledge of the project. Now with the FBI in on this whole thing, the cat is out of the bag."

"That makes it all the more imperative that we find your Dad."

"Yes, and I can thank them for that, but if and when they do, Dad's troubles might just be beginning."

After leaving Becky, he headed for Pence Technology. The office building was another twenty minutes away. It was located northwest of the Pence home in a commercial development on West Sixty-Second Street. As he pulled into the parking lot, he was surprised at the diminutive size of the building. It was only a single level structure of postmodern architecture. Contrary to the steel and glass material normally used for that period, it was built of red brick and granite, almost Spanish in design.

There were approximately a dozen cars in the front and on the side of the building. He found a space across from the entrance and parked. The glass door bore the Pence logo, the name Pence Technology, Incorporated and the street number, 6002. He pushed it open and walked to the receptionist's desk.

"May I help you?" the young lady asked without a smile.

"My name is Steve Gordon, and I'd like to see Dan Upstein."

"Sir, I'm not sure he'll be seeing anyone at this time. Our company experienced a terrible tragedy last evening."

Before Steve could respond, Janet Taylor appeared from the entrance to the offices. Her face was swollen and her eyes red.

"Mr. Gordon, I saw you come in." She took him by the arm and pulled him aside.

"Bill Chenowith was killed in an automobile accident last night." She choked as the tears welled in her eyes.

"My God!" Steve was visibly shaken. "How did it happen?"

Janet nodded at the receptionist and led Steve through the office door toward her office.

"We're not sure. The police say that a truck pushed Bill's car through a red light, and another truck with the green light hit him broad side. He was killed instantly."

Janet's desk was located in the small reception area outside of Gerald Pence's office. Across from the desk was a couch where Janet motioned Steve to sit. The office door was closed, but Steve heard voices from within. Janet followed his stare as she joined him on the couch.

"Dan Upstein is in there with a police detective investigating the accident."

"Have any of the officials on our case been notified of this?" Steve inquired.

"Not to my knowledge," Janet replied, bringing a Kleenex to her eyes.

"Mr. Gordon, there's something not right about this. I . . . I . . . I don't think Bill's death was an accident!"

"What do you mean?" he returned.

"I'm sure he knew more about all of this than he was telling us. I think someone didn't want him to tell what he knew."

"What are you saying?"

"The person who rear-ended Bill sped off, and they're still looking for him. I think this person deliberately hit Bill with the intent of killing him. Mr. Gordon, I think Bill Chenowith was murdered!"

"Steve, what the hell has gotten into you?" Doc Ewing barked over the phone. "I want you back here right now! The FBI guys know about Chenowith, and Sergeant Wilson has alerted the police up there, so there's nothing more you can do. Get your butt back here so I can wring your neck!"

"Doc, what's happening up here is related to our situation down there!" Steve pleaded. "We still haven't found Pence. We haven't found the missing hunters—if they ever existed. Now one of the principles in all this is dead, and it all started in our park. I think we have an obligation to stay involved."

There was silence on the other end of the line.

"Doc, are you there?" Steve inquired.

"Steve, I'm ordering you to come back down here right now," Doc replied in a suppressed voice.

"Okay, okay, Doc, you win." Steve mocked defeat. "But I've got to find Carolyn and check out of the hotel."

"Do that, Steve. And please . . . no more stunts."

Steve smiled as he hung up. Of course, Doc, he thought. No stunts. But it will take some time to find Carolyn. The Circle City Mall is a big place and Lord knows where she'll be.

Janet interrupted his ruminating.

"Mr. Upstein wants to talk to you, Steve. He's still in Pence's office."

Steve nodded and moved toward the door. "It didn't take him long to move into Pence's office did it?"

"I'm afraid you've come at a very inopportune time, Mr. Gordon."

Dan Upstein motioned for Steve to sit in one of the two chairs in front of the desk. He obliged and as he did, he took a quick visual tour of the office.

White . . . everything was white. The desk, with a chrome frame had a white laminated top. The walls, adorned with several large framed photographs of contemporary fighter jets, were white, and around the perimeter were white countertops with white cabinets below. The floor was white and light gray, checkered tile. In contrast to this stark white motif was what appeared to be a small steel-gray mainframe computer behind the desk. There was an additional personal computer on the desk and two more on the counters to the left, below two counter-to-ceiling windows. Open Venetian blinds did not obstruct the daylight, which exaggerated the almost blinding glow of the space. Aside from all this, the office was basically plain—truly a creation of a no-frills genius.

As Steve's instantaneous inspection of the office began to return to Dan Upstein, his eye caught sight of a briefcase on the floor below the far window. He caught the initials GRP.

Steve cleared his throat.

"I can understand," he said. "I was shocked to hear about Chenowith. What a freak accident!"

Upstein shifted nervously.

"Yes . . . yes it was. Gordon, as you can understand there are a lot of arrangements to be made. I don't have much time. To what do we owe this surprise visit?"

Steve pulled out his notebook and flipped briefly through it.

"If you don't mind, Mr. Upstein, I'd like to clear up a few questions I have on my mind."

Upstein's face reddened. "Good God, man, you kept us down there for three days asking questions. What in hell more could you want to know? And besides, by whose authority do you carry on this interrogation up here?"

Steve suppressed a smile. Hysteria again?, he thought.

"Sir, Gerald Pence—your president—disappeared while on the property of Williams Creek State Park. Things like this don't reflect well on us, and we have every right to attempt to get to the bottom of it any way we can," Steve retorted.

He hoped that his response would deflect the question of authority, which Steve knew he did not have. It occurred to him, suddenly, that his brazen actions were something he should have given more thought to.

Upstein cooled down.

"Okay, okay. What else do you want to know?"

Steve leaned back in his chair and contemplated the man before him for several seconds. Hell, he thought, I'm in hot water as it is. I might as well go for broke.

"Well for starters, Mr. Upstein, I find it inconceivable that a man in your position in this company could be so unaware of what was going on."

"You're referring to the sale of the company I suppose."

"Exactly."

Upstein folded the fingers of his hands in front of him and smiled faintly.

"If you knew Gerald Pence, you might not find it so inconceivable, Mr. Gordon. Pence was an extremely secretive person. As you found out at the lodge the other day, only Bill Chenowith knew about the proposed sale."

"So it would appear from the way you both reacted."

"I think that was a warranted reaction under the circumstances!"

"Agreed. You say that Gerald Pence was very secretive. How much did you know about this experimental aircraft he was working on?"

"I think I told you the other day that he talked about it when I was with him the night before he disappeared." Upstein was almost condescending in tone.

"Did it have anything to do with the proposed sale of your company?" Steve asked, crossing out a note in his book.

"Since the proposed buyer is a manufacturer of aircraft, I would imagine that it had quite a bit to do with the sale." He glanced at his watch. "I don't mean to be rude, Mr. Gordon, but as you know we suffered a great loss last night, and I am obligated to tend to the problems it has caused."

"Yes, I understand, and that leads me to another question. Do you think Chenowith's death was an accident?"

Upstein's dark eyes flashed. "What do you mean?"

"Mr. Upstein, a lot of things have happened in the last couple of days that don't seem to make sense. First, Pence disappears from his room in the park lodge. No one seems to know why. Second, we learn that your company was in the process of being sold without you, the executive vice president, knowing about it. Third, we find out that the man representing the prospective buyer of your company is having an affair with Pence's wife. If that's not enough, we learn through the FBI that the two left the country prior to Pence's disappearance, which would seem to eliminate them as suspects. Finally, Chenowith is suddenly killed in an accident that could be described as very bizarre."

Upstein fought to restrain himself. His face reddened again.

"I've been over all that with a police detective just as you popped in, Gordon. It was his thought that Chenowith was a victim of a hit-and-run, and, yes, it was terribly bizarre. Now, I must insist that we end this conversation." He rose to emphasize his point.

Steve stood as well and put his notebook back in his pocket. He pointed to the briefcase on the floor under the windows.

"Oh, I almost forgot. I seem to remember that it was determined that Pence's briefcase had disappeared along with him. I notice that that one over there has the initials GRP on it. Would it be—?"

"Gerald Pence had several briefcases," Upstein said, interrupting. "That happens to be one of them."

There was a knock on the door. It opened and two men entered. One was tall and husky and may have weighed in at 250. The other was short and slight and carried his right arm in a sling. They both wore dark suits and ties.

Upstein smiled and walked from behind the desk toward them.

"Gentlemen, this is Mr. Steve Gordon from the Williams Creek State Park. He was just leaving. Would you be so kind as to escort him to his car?"

He turned to Steve.

"It's been a delight, Mr. Gordon. I wouldn't worry too much about this. I'm sure you have more than your share of worries at the park."

Steve felt hands on his arms and a mild push toward the door. They moved through the reception area toward the hallway. Janet looked up nervously from her desk.

"Is there anything I can help you with, Mr. Gordon?"

Steve hesitated and pulling away from the grips of the two men, reached in his pocket and pulled out his notebook. He wrote something down; ripped out the page and handed it to Janet.

"Yes, Ms. Taylor, if you would call my wife at this number and tell her I'm on my way, I'd appreciate it."

Janet was confused by the expression on Steve's face, but took the note.

"I'd be happy to," she said without looking at the piece of paper.

"Thanks," he said as his escorts renewed their grips and led him into the hall and out the main door to the parking lot.

"What do you two do here?" he asked as they neared his car.

The husky man growled. "We're company security."

At the car, Steve turned to the smaller man. "What happened to your arm?"

The man looked passively at the sling and smiled. He responded in a startling high pitched voice. "I banged it up in a game of hand ball."

Steve got into his car and waved at the two men. "Thanks for showing me to my car. Maybe I'll see you both later."

They walked off toward a van parked at the side of the building but within his sight. Steve watched them intently as he started his engine.

That voice, he thought. Almost feminine. He slipped the car into gear, still eyeing the two men as they climbed into the van. He noticed the big man, now behind the wheel, watching him through the side view mirror, so he moved the car slowly toward the parking lot entrance. He pulled out and turned right. Through the rear view mirror he saw the van leave the lot and turn left. He immediately pulled into another parking lot further up the road and turned his car around. As he moved out, he could still see the van. As he followed at a safe distance, his mind began to dwell on the small man's voice. Suddenly, he remembered the night of the fire fight at the park and what the wounded Bob Zimmerman had said.

"During the exchange of fire up there, one of them shouted something to the other, Steve. I could swear it sounded like a woman!" and earlier, at the top of the hill he had said, "I think I hit one of them!" That voice; the arm in a sling. By God, he thought as he kept the van in sight, I've found the two hunters!

Janet Taylor looked at the piece of paper Steve had handed her. "In fifteen minutes, call me on my cell phone, 812-833-7569."

CHAPTER 7

ergeant Wilson sat in the park office in front of a fidgety Doc Ewing. Doc played with an empty Styrofoam coffee cup and stared at the phone on his desk in front of him. He glanced at his watch. It had been almost an hour since his conversation with Steve Gordon.

"Do you think Gordon will follow your orders?" Wilson asked with a half-smile.

"What! Sherlock Holmes follow orders? Hell no!" Doc shot back.

"I thought he was going up there to do some Christmas shopping." Doc heartily tossed the coffee cup into the wastepaper basket by the filing cabinet.

"Another one of his clever tricks. I should have seen through this right off."

"He's treading on thin ice, Doc."

Doc looked sharply at the sergeant. "Hell, Al, don't you think I know that? I ought to go up there right now and kick his butt all the way back here!"

Wilson chuckled.

"You know what I think?" Ewing continued. "I think those two in the Caymans are still involved somehow. I don't know in what way, but they're involved."

"Could be, Doctor Watson," Allen retorted with a smile. He settled back in his chair and looked at Doc soberly.

"We'll know fairly soon. The FBI has notified the authorities down there. They're to pick them up and have them extradited back here."

Doc rose from his desk and moved to the window. It had snowed lightly during the night, and there was a fresh layer of white on the ground. He turned toward the sergeant.

"Do you realize that Christmas is only twelve days away?"

"Not much time left to do your shopping, is there, Doc?"

"I hear the shopping is great in the Circle City," Ewing mused.

Sergeant Wilson reached for the phone. He dialed and looked over at Doc. "How much have you forgotten about flying a helicopter?"

"Not a thing, Al. Not a thing." He smiled.

Steve's cell phone rang. He picked it up with his free hand. "Janet?"

"Yes, Steve."

"Can you talk?"

"Yes. Mr. Upstein left Gerald Pence's office about ten minutes ago."

"Okay. I agree with you, Janet. There is something very strange going on here, and I think I'm beginning to understand what it is. I'm following the two security guys. We're heading toward Zionsville Road. Any idea where we're going?"

"Probably going to our warehouse."

Janet's voice began to quiver.

"We keep supplies and production materials there along with other odds and ends."

"Anything else?"

"I haven't been there for a long time, Steve. In fact, we have been specifically told that the warehouse is off limits to all office personnel indefinitely."

"Strange." Steve watched the car ahead turn north on Zionsville Road. He fell back and let them disappear temporarily before he, too, made the turn. He knew now that they were close to their destination.

"Listen to me, Janet. That briefcase in Pence's office . . . is it the one that was missing at the park lodge?"

"I don't know, Steve. I didn't get that good a look at it. But it makes no difference now. Mr. Upstein was carrying it with him when he left. I think he's headed your way."

"Okay. Are you willing to do something that might be dangerous?"

"Yes, Yes, Steve, anything."

"Go into Chenowith's office and turn it upside-down. Look for anything that will give us a clue as to why he might have been murdered."

"Alright. Shall I call you back if I find anything?"

"No, No! I'm going to turn my phone off. I don't want it going off at the wrong time. I'll get back to you. Be careful."

Steve buttoned off and set the phone on the car seat beside him. The car ahead now turned into a parking lot in front of a row of four massive, beige-colored warehouses.

It pulled up to the forth structure from the road to one of two large, sliding garage doors. One opened, and the car drove in and disappeared as the door closed behind it. Steve pulled into a lot adjacent to the Pence warehouse. He parked facing the building and turned the engine off. He glanced at his watch. It was one fifteen in the afternoon. He still had time to follow through here and get back to the park as ordered.

He scanned the outside of the building. There was one window on each side of the large sliding doors and a small entranceway to the left. Along the left side of the building, which was the only side he was able to see from his vantage point, were two more windows. If he could approach the structure from the left across a stretch of intervening grass, he would be unseen. He could then reach the first window and get a good look at the building's interior. He eased the car door open, scrutinizing the area carefully as he did. He stepped out and gently pushed the door closed. So far so good.

Steve walked across the open grassy area trying not to be conspicuous to passing traffic. He reached the first window and flattened himself against the metal side to the right of it. Slowly he eased his head around to the window pane and looked in. The window was behind racks of shelves loaded with boxes and crates. There were enough openings for him to identify the van in the center area and behind it a series of vaults with what appeared to be metal doors. The two men were nowhere to be seen. It occurred to Steve that if there were windows on the other side of the building like the ones on this side, he might be able to see into the vaults. He surveyed the area to make sure that he was still unobserved and then proceeded around the back of the building to the other side. He entered the small space between the buildings and approached the first window. It revealed only more shelving. He crept toward the other window and started to peer in when a voice from behind startled him.

"Fancy meeting you here, Mr. Gordon!"

Before he could turn fully around, a sharp blow to his head sent him into black oblivion.

Janet hung up the phone after her conversation with Steve. She sat momentarily gathering her thoughts. Ransacking Gerald Pence's office would be one thing. After all, she was his secretary. But going into Bill Chenowith's office to nose around would be something else. What if Bill's secretary should appear? She certainly would object. Maybe if she waited until after office hours when everyone had gone home. No, Steve's request seemed urgent. She'd have to do it now. She drew a deep breath and rose from her desk. Chenowith's office was at the end of the hall from her reception area. She walked the distance and stopped in front of the closed office door. As she reached for the door knob, she hesitated. There were voices coming from inside.

Janet stepped back and debated whether to return to her desk or proceed. After a moment, she opened the door and entered.

The company's chief legal officer, Dean Marshall sat behind Chenowith's desk in front of his computer. Mary Davis, the company human resources director, stood in front of an open filing cabinet against the wall to the right of the desk. For a moment there was shocked silence as Janet stared at the two and they at her. Dean was the first to speak.

"What can we do for you, Janet?"

Janet hesitated in embarrassment. What could she say?

"Are you wondering what we're doing here?" Mary smiled.

There was more silence. Janet felt she was in a corner, so why not tell it all—now!

"I came here to look around. I came here to find anything that would tell me why Bill Chenowith was killed."

Dean walked from behind the desk to the door of the office and closed it. He approached Janet pensively. Mary remained at the filing cabinet.

"Are you saying that you don't think Bills death was an accident?"

Janet swallowed hard. "That's what I'm saying!"

Dean looked at Mary and then back to Janet. "Well, welcome to the club."

When Steve regained consciousness he found himself in what appeared to be a dimly lighted vault. No windows. Concrete walls. As he attempted to bring his right hand up to his throbbing head, he realized that he was handcuffed to a pipe that ran the length of the wall. He sat up trying to adjust his eyes to the bleak lighting. There was a cot across from him. Beside the cot was a table, which bore the hurricane lamp that provided what little illumination there was. On the cot sat a man, slumped forward, hands draped between his knees and with invisible eyes staring at Steve. He could barely make out the individual's features. What he saw was haggard and bearded with at least several days' growth. There was a severe abrasion on his right temple. The figure spoke with a raspy croak.

"Who . . . who are you?"

"My name is Steve Gordon, from the state park in Williams County."

For a moment Steve thought he might lose consciousness again, but he fought it off. He focused his attention on the figure across from him. He was of average build which was diminished by his decrepit condition. His unkempt white hair hung over sunken eyes and framed a long, narrow face.

In a halting voice Steve said, "Mr. Gerald Pence I presume."

Allen Wilson spoke through his headset mic. "How does it handle, Doc? Like a Huey?"

Doc wiggled the control column and laughed. "Hell no! It's like flying a kite compared to that elephant."

The state police had delivered a Bell 206B helicopter to the landing site outside the park headquarters after Wilson's call. At Wilson's request and assurances that Doc Ewing was qualified, the trooper pilot turned the helicopter over to them. Moments later, they were in the air and headed north toward Indianapolis.

"Do you know where Pence Technology is?" Allen shouted into the mic over the hum of the 'copter engine.

Doc pointed down to the 750 NAV screen between the two seats. "This little baby will take us right to it."

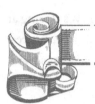

CHAPTER 8

J anet was appalled. "I can't believe what you're telling me." She stood behind Dean Marshall sitting at Chenowith's desk and stared in disbelief at what she saw on the computer screen in front of them. Mary Davis, standing beside Janet shook her head.

"Quite frankly, it doesn't surprise me that Dan Upstein might do this, but it's hard to believe that Chenowith was involved."

Dean looked up at Davis.

"We're not sure he was, Mary, but I can't believe that as the chief financial officer, he couldn't see what was happening to the inventory."

Janet was confused. She drew her head closer to the computer screen. "What am I looking at?"

Dean pointed to a set of figures.

"This column shows the number of legitimate sales of computer chips by month for all of last year. This column shows what the inventory should be for the same period. This next column rings the bell! It shows what a recent audit tells us the actual inventory is."

There was silence as the implication of what Janet was looking at sunk in.

"My God." She gasped. "There's almost a difference of three hundred units!"

"Nearly five hundred thousand dollars' worth." Dean answered.

"Dan Upstein was bootlegging our microprocessors?" Janet choked on her words.

"Dan Upstein was responsible for the procurement of material for the manufacture and inventorying of the processors. He was the only one with access and opportunity."

"And we think Bill Chenowith was either in on it, or he discovered the discrepancy and confronted Upstein," Mary added.

"Or he didn't confront Upstein, but was planning to tell Pence!" Dean continued.

The light dawned on Janet.

"So to silence Chenowith, Upstein set up his accident."

Mary crossed over to Janet, her arms folded across her chest. "And we think he had something to do with Gerald Pence's disappearance."

Janet felt faint. "Oh my God! That means that Steve Gordon is in grave danger."

Dean jumped to his feet. "What do you mean, Janet?"

"Steve Gordon paid a visit to Upstein a little while ago and it was obvious that it didn't go well. He was escorted out of the office by those two security thugs Upstein hired. He slipped me a note asking me to call him in fifteen minutes and I did. He was following those two jerks to the warehouse."

"And?"

"I think that's where Upstein is headed. Steve could be in real trouble."

Dean walked from behind the desk and grabbed both Mary and Janet by the arms as he headed toward the office door.

"Not could be, Janet . . . is!"

The sound of a helicopter reached their ears as they hurried down the hall.

"They've been drugging me ever since I've been here." Gerald Pence shook his head in an effort to clear it. "I don't know how many times they've done it, but enough to keep me like this."

Steve was listening, but he also was assessing the room for any possibilities of escape. He studied the pipe that he was handcuffed to. He had to do something to break it and free himself. But what if it was a gas pipe! In this vault it could be fatal to the both of them. He scrutinized the walls and the ceiling. On the ceiling in the far corner was a large air vent which looked like an exit possibility. In frustration, he jerked violently at the handcuff to no avail. He had to find a way!

Steve turned his attention to Gerald.

"Do you have any idea at all when they'll be back?"

"I'm afraid not." Gerald hung his head.

His gaze returned to the pipe. It was about a foot from the floor and an inch and a half away from the wall, and it was about an inch in diameter. With the proper leverage, Steve realized that a good kick might break it. He felt it with his free hand. It was cold, suggesting that it could be a water pipe. A broken water pipe wouldn't be an immediate danger to them.

Gerald watched Steve intently, still fighting off the effects of the drug he had been given.

"What is your involvement in all of this?" his voice was weak and scratchy.

Steve was startled by the question. "You do remember Williams Creek County and the state park?"

Pence responded hesitantly. "Y-yes. We were going to have a meeting. I was with Dan Upstein the night before in his room at the lodge. We had an argument . . ."

"An argument?! Upstein told us that you two were drinking pretty heavily and that all you talked about was your XSA project," Steve responded.

"Bullshit! Yes, we had a drink or two, but we had a damn fight over the sale of the company."

Steve shook his head in disbelief.

"So he did know about the sale before your trip to the park."

"He and Chenowith both knew about it and they were both against it. The others down there, as far as I know, were clueless. I was going to lay it on them at the meeting."

Steve looked at his watch, which, to his amazement, they hadn't taken. It had been approximately twenty-five minutes since he regained consciousness. He sensed that time was running out.

"Mr. Pence, we have a lot to talk about, but right now we've got to attend to important business—like getting the hell out of here." Steve gripped the pipe. There was little give. The firmer the better he thought. He looked over to Pence. "Can you help me here?"

He motioned him over to the pipe and pointed to a spot below where he held it. Pence gingerly followed instructions. At that moment, the sound of a key in the door lock froze them.

Doc set the helicopter down on the Tarmac parking lot in front of Pence Technology. Allen Wilson jumped out and ran toward the three people standing anxiously by the entrance.

"Thank God you're here!" Janet screamed above the whirl of the copter, "We've got to get to our warehouse right away. I don't have time to explain now, but we think Steve Gordon is in serious trouble!"

Allen stuck his head in close to the three. He looked at Dean and Mary.

"Ms. Taylor will come with us. You two call the FBI office here and tell them what's happening!"

He grabbed Janet by the arm and guided her beneath the spinning blades. He helped her into the rear seat of the helicopter and boarded it himself. Doc raised the pitch lever lifting the craft off the asphalt and, once clear of the trees and buildings, pushed the control column forward. They were on their way to the warehouse.

Agent Kyle Broyles sat in his Indianapolis office talking by phone to Agent Manning in Chicago.

"Chenowith's death might not be a coincidence, Kyle, when you hear about our Cayman couple. This comes from our agents down there."

Broyles rose from his desk and began pacing the office.

Manning continued. "They traced them to the Owen Roberts Airport in Grand Cayman on the afternoon of December 9."

"At the time of Pence's disappearance," Kyle said.

"Right!" Manning went on. "They checked into the Westin Casuarina under the name of John W. Barry. The next morning, they tracked Atkins to an offshore bank in George Town. After that, the two went scuba diving in West Bay."

"Did they find out what he was doing at the offshore bank?" Broyles asked.

"They pulled the 'Confidential Law' on them. They couldn't get anything out of them. Obviously there was some kind of deposit involved."

Kyle chuckled. "Laundry?"

"Sounds like it," Manning said. "But there's more! Atkins shook us. He just disappeared."

"What about the gal?"

"Her body was found floating face down in bay. The authorities say it looked like an accidental drowning."

"Accidental drowning!?" Kyle shouted. "Didn't your guys tell them about Atkins?"

Manning pulled the phone from his ear. His voice phased back in.

"Hey, take it easy, man. Yes, they did, but they said there was nothing to prove that it was other than an accident."

Kyle sat back down at his desk.

"Okay, so what's next?"

"They checked the bookings at the airport, but there was nothing under the names of either Barry or Atkins. He must have used another alias, or he hired a private flight out . . . or he's still somewhere on the island."

"What do you think?"

"I think . . . if he didn't drown too . . . he probably hired a private plane out and is working his way back here. We're staking out the airports up here."

Kyle rested the phone on the desk in thought.

"You still there?" Manning asked.

He pulled the phone back. "You know, Chuck, I just happened to think. Pence is missing, maybe even dead. His wife drowns, and Chenowith is killed, both under very mysterious circumstances, and we don't know if this Atkins guy is dead or alive. If he's alive and his motives are what I think they might be, Becky Pence may be in danger."

"How do you figure that?"

"There's something big going on here. I think it's apparent that Atkins has got a big stake in Pence's company, and it's also apparent that he and someone or maybe several someones inside the company are hiding something. Two people who might have known what that is are dead. We don't know how much Becky Pence knows, but neither does Atkins or his cohorts. If they did in Chenowith and her mother for that reason, she could be next for the same reason."

Kyle's secretary entered his office. She motioned for his attention. "Mr. Broyles, there's an urgent message on line two from a Dean Marshall of Pence Technology."

CHAPTER 9

"Get back on the cot and act like you're still out," Steve whispered.

Pence followed orders and Steve lay down by the wall, feigning unconsciousness. The vault door opened and out of the corner of his eye, he saw the figure of the small man. The beam of a flashlight darted first at the still form of Gerald and then to Steve. After a slight hesitation, the figure moved toward the cot. Steve thought, another shot. Mustn't allow it. He moaned. The figure turned and came toward him. It leaned closer to his supine form. Steve suddenly raised both legs and with all his strength drove both feet to the figure's head. There was the sound of crunching bone and a shriek as the figure fell against the door, slamming it shut, and then crumbled to the floor.

Gerald sat up and stared at the still form. "What a shot! You might have killed the bastard."

"Look for keys." Steve pointed toward the still form.

Pence rose and picked up the flashlight lying beside the figure. He frisked the jacket pockets.

"Here they are—a key ring with several keys on it."

"Find a key that looks like it might fit these cuffs," Steve said. Gerald complied and after sliding several keys around the ring, he smiled.

"Yes, this looks like the one." He slid over to Steve and fitted the key into the handcuff. He turned it, and the handcuffs popped open.

"I can't believe our luck," Steve said, rubbing the circulation back into his wrist. "Now let's get out of here." He moved to the door but recoiled.

"Good God, the door opens from the outside! We're still locked in."

"What about him!? He'll wake up soon," Gerald said.

Steve took the flashlight from Pence and beamed it around until it fell on a syringe lying on the floor by the cot.

"This was meant for you, but I think it's only proper that we needle our friend here a little."

Steve picked it up and, with a swift motion, injected the contents into the unconscious man's arm.

"This will keep him quiet for a while."

Pence sat on the cot. "Okay, now what?"

Without answering, Steve walked over to the corner of the vault and flashed the light up at the air vent in the ceiling. He removed the kerosene lamp from the table and set it on the floor.

"Help steady this thing," he said to Gerald.

He raised himself onto the table and stood up facing the vent grill as Pence held tightly to the table sides. He swooned slightly, his head still throbbing. Steve suspected he had a mild concussion. He steadied himself. He was now almost at eye level with the vent. He pushed the grill up, slid it to the side within the duct work, and examined its interior with the flashlight. It was circular, about three feet in diameter. There was room for a man his size to fit through. He gripped both sides of the opening and struggled up and into the duct. Twisting his body lengthwise, he looked down the stretch of pipe. It was a maze of ductwork that apparently branched off to other parts of the building. He looked down through the vent opening.

"I don't think you can make it up here," he whispered. "There's a network of ducts that look like they cover the rest of the building. There's got to be other vents away from the vaults. Hand me the keys."

Gerald lifted them up to Steve.

"I'll have you out of there in no time."

Steve labored through the duct to a junction that shot to the left toward the center of the warehouse. He twisted his body into it and slid forward to another vent cover that overlooked what appeared to be a truck bed. Sliding the cover gently away from him, he thrust his head down through the opening. He could see two figures in the glassed-in office to his right, the truck below him, and the blue van to his left. He was clear.

Dan Upstein sat at the desk in the glassed-in office in the corner of the warehouse adjacent to the row of vaults. The larger thug sat across from him by the office door cleaning his fingernails with a pen knife. On the desk was an open briefcase and a spread of documents. Upstein reached over, picked one up, and studied it. It was a sketch of the XSA—Pence's dream child. He toyed with his beard in thought. How could this thing fly? Did Atkins really think it was worth all this effort? If he were here, he might be able to justify all this. But he wasn't, and this aggravated Upstein. Where was he?

It had been four days since he had given Atkins the suitcase containing the money. His mission had been the same as the other two involving the Caymans. Deposit it to an offshore bank for shipment to Switzerland. He flipped the drawing back on the desk in disgust. He couldn't understand it anyway. He thought of Bill Chenowith. He was truly sorry he had to do what he did, but Chenowith was about to blow the whistle. As it was, the jig could well be up anyway, and what had been deposited thus far would have to do. Upstein half smiled. Over five million and three quarter dollars would do him for quite a while. Atkins would, of course, get his share, but what was left would be more than adequate. Then a thought occurred to him. He picked up a pencil and began tapping it nervously on the desk top. What if Atkins had deposited all the money in a different name than Dan had given him?! He had been presented receipts, but they could be faked. Would he put it past that son of a bitch? He tossed the pencil down and dropped back heavily in his chair. Would Atkins do that? He glanced at his watch. He should have heard from him by now. The normal routine was a phone call after each trip. Something was wrong. Then he thought of Steve Gordon locked up in the vault with Pence. He would have to dispose of him somehow. He shook his head. This whole thing was getting too complicated.

He looked over at the big security man by the door.

"When Pete gets back, I want you two to wrap that Gordon guy up nice and tight and get rid of him."

"Where?"

"Anywhere were they won't find him until spring." He glanced at his watch again. "What's taking Pete so long? Go see."

Slipping through the opening, Steve eased himself onto the truck bed and then to the concrete floor. He moved to the front of the truck toward the four vault doors. Pence had to be in the second vault to his right. He nervously fumbled through the keys on the ring until he came to one that he was sure would opened the door. He looked about. Still clear. He dashed for the door, inserted the key and twisted. He swung the door open. Pence stood trying to adjust his eyes to the sudden light.

"Let's go!" Steve whispered.

Just as they reached the truck, the office door opened, and the big man emerged. They swung to the opposite side of the vehicle and watched as the security guard approached the open vault.

"We've got to get to the front exit," Steve said in a hushed voice, "When that guy reaches the vault, he's going to be one pissed-off camper."

The two ran toward the far side of the building using the truck to shield them. Half way there, Pence kicked a loose pipe that lay on the floor and sent it clattering up against the metal shelving.

"Shit!" Pence shouted.

Steve grabbed his arm. "Get to the door, quick!"

The big man froze at the vault door and then spun around toward the center of the warehouse. He drew his pistol and moved cautiously to the vehicles. He heard the running footsteps and hurried forward. Pence and Gordon reached the door and desperately tried to pull it open. It was locked! A shot and the ping of a ricochet off one of the shelves echoed throughout the warehouse. The big man rounded the truck and confronted the two huddled by the door. He moved toward them, a forty-five leveled their way and a smirk on his face.

"You really didn't think you were going to get away?"

Upstein's office door swung open, and he dashed out.

"What the hell is going on here?" Upstein bellowed.

The big man motioned with his pistol for the two to move toward him. Upstein approached his side, with a look of shock on his face.

"Things are catching up with you, Upstein," Steve barked.

His composure returning, Upstein motioned for the big man to lower his gun. "Whatever do you mean, Mr. Gordon?"

"You know what he means, you bastard," Pence retorted. "You had me kidnapped by this idiot and your other flunky and have had me drugged up for the past four days."

"Not to mention Chenowith," Steve added.

Pence turned to Steve. "What about Chenowith?"

"I didn't have the chance to tell you, Gerald, but Bill Chenowith was killed yesterday evening."

Pence's face went white.

Steve turned his attention to Upstein. "And I have every reason to believe this gentleman had something to do with it."

Upstein chuckled. "That, you'll have a problem proving, my friend."

"Your complicity in the kidnapping shouldn't be hard to prove," Steve returned.

Upstein moved toward Steve.

"You forget, Mr. Gordon, you are hardly in a position to prove anything. Now, I would assume that our little friend is locked up in your vault, so I will ask you to kindly hand over the keys." As Upstein extended his hand, the phone rang in his office. He froze. He shook his hand impatiently at the two. "The keys . . . the keys!"

The phone rang again. He turned his head toward the sound. Could this be the call from Atkins? Who else knew he was here. The phone continued to ring. Resigned, he cast a glance over at the big man.

"I'm expecting this call," he said, moving toward the office. "Get the keys and put these gentlemen back in the vault!"

As he approached the office door, the ringing stopped. Upstein was too late. Disgusted, he plopped into the swivel chair behind his desk and pushed the playback button on the blinking answering machine. It was Atkins's voice.

"I left a long message on your machine at your office. It'll explain everything. I'll talk to you later."

Upstein paled as he pushed himself away from the desk. Good God, he thought. What has that damn fool said on the machine??

He rose and dashed to the office door. He had to get to his office . . . now! As he ran onto the floor of the warehouse, the sound of an approaching helicopter and screeching car brakes echoed throughout, halting him momentarily. A hand grabbed his shoulder. He spun about and looked into the eyes of Steve Gordon who was straddling the supine form of the big man.

"Sorry about your man here, who incidentally is not the brightest light in the harbor. He got a little distracted when I tossed the keys his way. You didn't really think we were going back into that damn vault did you?"

CHAPTER 10

Mary Davis had taken Atkins's message off Upstein's machine, and in a state of shock, had called Agent Broyles on his cell phone to tell him of its contents.

"Don't let anyone touch that machine!" he had said. We'll be there in about half an hour."

Agent Broyles, Sergeant Wilson, Doc Ewing, Janet Taylor, and Steve stood huddled around Upstein's desk. The handcuffed Upstein sat in his desk chair, white faced and perspiring heavily. Atkins's voice issued from the telephone answering machine.

"Sorry I'm so late, but a few things have happened down here. Some of them you might be better off not hearing about, but I'm going to tell you anyway. I took Darlene down here with me. I figured you wouldn't care."

Upstein shook his head in disgust.

"She got to be a problem, Upstein. I had to get rid of her."

The group exchanged shocked expressions.

"So now, I've got to lay low. The money's deposited. I took out what I thought was my share. I still want those plans you promised me, and I'll hold you to it! I'll be in touch. Adios."

Everyone was silent for a brief moment.

Janet asked, "Does Gerald know about his wife?"

Agent Broyles responded, "I told him after we apprehended these guys. In the condition he was in, I don't think it registered."

Sergeant Wilson leaned toward the slumping Upstein.

"Well, Mr. Upstein, it's all pretty conclusive. Do you have anything to add?"

Upstein twisted nervously in his chair. He dropped his head. "I am not responsible for anything that man has said or done."

"And the other charges?" Wilson continued.

Upstein looked up sardonically. "I'll say no more until I talk to my attorney."

Steve spoke up. "Maybe you'll answer this one: it should be obvious by now that Porter Aviation's board of directors has booted their illicit CEO. What could he do with the XSA plans? Build it in his garage?"

Another smirk followed. "Mr. Gordon, I would have no idea. I had no interest in that Mickey Mouse project."

Sergeant Wilson went informal and leaned back in his chair. "Off the record, Upstein. Why?"

"Why?"

"You and guys like you have had it reasonably good. Good position, good income . . . life by the balls! Yet, you screw up with stupid things like this. Why?"

Upstein chuckled. "Life by the balls, Sergeant? By your standards, maybe I had it all. What kind of life do you have? What would you really do to live the life you think I do, Sergeant? How much would it take to have you break the law? $50,000? $100,000? $500,000? As they say, everyone has his price, Sergeant!"

Wilson's face paled. "Guys like you really believe that crap! You haven't answered my question."

Upstein became vehement. "The company was in shambles. All because of Pence's stupid obsession with a dream. It was all going down anyway, so why not get what I could before it did. When Atkins got into the act, I couldn't believe my good fortune. A drunken, two-timing wife, a ruthless swindler, and an idealistic idiot . . . it was perfect! As a result, I've banked more money than I would have ever seen by having . . . as you put it, sergeant, 'life by the balls'!"

Steve sat on the edge of the desk, his arms folded, looking down with disdain.

"Was murder part of the scheme?"

"That was an accident!" Upstein shot back.

"Not according to your cronies."

Upstein leaned back smugly. "It's their word against mine."

The receptionist stuck her head into Upstein's office.

"Sergeant Wilson, they're here to take him away."

Wilson looked toward the door. "Send them in." He turned back to Upstein. "I would suggest that you call your lawyer when you reach the station, Mr. Upstein. That way you can spend all the time you need filling him in when he gets there. Tell him to bring a tape recorder. He couldn't possibly digest it all in one sitting."

Pence sat on the couch in the great room of his home flanked by his daughter and Janet Taylor. Across from them were Sergeant Wilson, Doc Ewing, and Agent Broyles. Steve stood by the back windows.

Pence patted his newly bandaged head. "This happened when Upstein's thugs burst into my room at the lodge. The big guy had a gun with a silencer. We wrestled; the thing went off, and that's all I remember until I woke up in their van, bound and gagged. That's when they started with the drugs."

"Were you awake at the shootout at Sharon Lake?" Wilson asked.

"No! When my head began to clear I was in the vault at the warehouse."

"Any idea how long you'd been there?" Doc interjected.

"I lost all track of time. It seemed like an eternity. Every time I woke up, they'd shoot me up again."

He motioned behind him to Steve. "Then they brought this guy in. He was in worse shape than me."

Steve grinned and rubbed his head. "My head seems to be a target these days."

Agent Broyles produced a tape recorder from his briefcase and laid it on the coffee table in front of him. "I hope you don't mind us tape recording this, Mr. Pence. For the record."

"No, it's fine." He nodded.

Broyles continued. "What, in your opinion, were the motives behind all this?"

Gerald smiled stoically. "Hell, I don't know. Greed mostly, I suppose. I think the problem began to develop when I considered the possibility of selling the company.

I put out feelers about a year ago, and shortly after that, Porter Aviation and Daryl Atkins appeared on the scene. I don't know why Dan Upstein pretended not to know about all this, because he did. I told him that night at the lodge. That's why we argued."

Steve strolled around the couch and stood in the center of the group. "Why wouldn't he? According to what Chenowith said, nobody but he and you knew about the sale. When you told Upstein that night, he decided to take immediate steps to get you out of the picture. The next day, he denied knowledge of the sale to eliminate himself as a suspect. I have to admit it was one hell of a piece of acting."

"Why was Chenowith murdered?" Gerald asked.

Janet Taylor spoke up. "Upstein was bootlegging computer chips from the company—hundreds of thousands of dollars' worth. Chenowith confronted him with documentation to that effect and, I suspect, threatened to blow the whistle. He panicked, and the night after Chenowith and I returned from Williams County, he arranged with his thugs to set up the 'accident.'"

They both confessed to it," said Sergeant Wilson. "They also fessed up to kidnapping Pence and implicated Upstein in both cases."

"That and the telephone tape sets up an ironclad case against Upstein."

Agent Broyles said, "But unfortunately Atkins is still missing."

The group suddenly grew silent as all eyes fell on Becky Pence on the couch. She bowed her head as Gerald reached over and took her hand.

"I'm sorry, honey. If you'd like to lie down for a while . . ."

"No, no! I'm all right," Becky whispered. "I want to hear everything."

They all took in her response.

Steve broke the silence. "Can I suggest a theory?"

Doc Ewing threw up his arms. "God, Sherlock Holmes strikes again!"

Steve ignored him. "Upstein offered Atkins a cut of the computer chip action if he and his company would drop the buy-out idea, and Atkins agreed if Upstein would get him the plans for the XSA."

Steve grew uncomfortable as he glanced toward Becky.

"Go ahead, Mr. Gordon, say it. My mother was the vehicle in this arrangement."

The air grew heavy. Gerald's voice was emotional as he addressed the group.

"My daughter has just lost her mother, gentlemen, I beg you to use a little discretion here."

Becky exploded, "It's all right, Dad!" She surveyed her audience and calmed down. "I lost my mother years ago!" She cast a sideward glance toward Gerald. "You know that, Dad."

Pence renewed his grasp of Becky's hand. "What my daughter is saying is that Atkins really had nothing to do with what happened to the relationship between her mother and me. That breakdown happened years ago, and I'll share a great part of the blame."

Becky dropped her head on Gerald's shoulder. "Oh, Daddy, don't say that."

"It's true, honey. Too many years of thinking my work was more important than relationships."

Agent Broyles leaned forward and turned the tape recorder off.

"I didn't have the time to spend working on your mother's happiness or with you for that matter. We grew further and further apart until our love for each other began to wane."

His attention now was fully on Becky. "That's when she began the heavy drinking and the wandering off at night. I grew even more frustrated, and what time I didn't spend at the office late at night, I spent locked up in my den here at the house."

Gerald clasped his hands between his legs. His head dropped. "That's when she became susceptible to Atkins's advances. At first it was flirtations when I took her with me to dinner meetings with him. Several instances here at the house opened my eyes to what was happening. I confronted her. She denied it. I confronted him. He denied it. Then the trips to Chicago began."

He looked deeply into Becky's tearing eyes. "All the time you were the one who bore the brunt of this. Your mother and I were selfishly squandering your life . . . your happiness. For that I will never be able to forgive myself."

Becky sobbed openly. There was an awkward silence in the room as eyes began studying shoes or fingernails.

Steve rubbed his chin and cleared his throat. "I don't think Upstein will figure that he has anything to lose by throwing the blame for all this on Atkins. It will be a different story, though, when we find him. It's pretty clear from all the evidence that Atkins was involved in Mrs. Pence's death."

Sergeant Wilson interjected and trailed off as he cast an embarrassed look toward Becky.

"It's all right." Becky smiled through her tears. "I'm a big girl. Please feel free to say what you think."

"Haven't they done any investigating down there?" Gerald asked.

"Not preliminarily," answered Kyle Broyles. "The local police called it an 'accidental drowning.'"

"But the guy disappeared!" Pence exploded. "Didn't that raise a few suspicions?"

Agent Broyles raised his hand to calm Gerald. "I've been in contact with the police commissioner in George Town. He said that indeed Atkins's flying the coop did raise some flags, and they have delayed returning the body here to conduct an autopsy. We haven't heard back."

Gerald shot to his feet, bolted to the fireplace, and turned. "In the meantime the son of a bitch walks around free!"

"Mr. Pence," Wilson said, "unless they can find something down there, they don't have anything they can legally hold him on here."

Steve shook his head. "What I don't understand in all this is what Atkins would do with the XSA plans if he got them."

Pence responded matter-of-factly, "Absolutely nothing!"

"Then why would he go to all this trouble?"

Doc Ewing rose to his feet, stretched, and looked over at Steve. "Well, Mr. Naturalist, I think we've contributed enough to the problems here. It's time to go back to the farm and do what we're paid to do"

Steve resisted. "Doc, Carolyn and I have gone past the checkout time at the hotel. Why not let us stay over until morning. Then we'll shoot right back."

"Oh no you don't. You're not pulling that on me again. What's going on up here is none of our business now. Your Christmas shopping is over and you and Carolyn are going back to Williams Creek tonight!"

"Doc, think of the money we're wasting," Steve pleaded.

Ewing walked over to Steve and poked his chest. "That won't work, Gordon. If I have to have Sergeant Wilson escort you back, that's what I'll do!"

Allen Wilson suppressed a laugh and Steve slumped in resignation.

"Okay, Doc, you win."

"God! Where have I heard that before?"

"I'm standing in front of the home of Mr. Gerald V. Pence, who just hours ago was rescued from abductors at a warehouse on Zionsville Road on the northwest side of Indianapolis. With him was Steve Gordon, naturalist at Williams Creek State Park in southern Indiana, who was part of the rescue team along with elements of the state and county police and the Federal Bureau of Investigation. Mr. Pence is currently inside the house with representatives of these authorities and is unavailable for comment. Arrested at the Zionsville Road warehouse was a Mr. Daniel Upstein, an executive at Gerald Pence's company, and two security guards. Mr. Upstein will be held on several counts, one as an accomplice in the alleged murder of Pence Technology CFO, William Chenowith.

Mr. Daryl Atkins, of the Porter Aviation Corporation in Chicago, was given as a coconspirator, but is at large at this time. It was also reported that the body of Gerald Pence's estranged wife was recovered on Grand Cayman Island in what authorities down there are initially reporting as a drowning accident. Since we understand that Daryl Atkins was with Mrs. Pence at the time, there is reason to believe that Atkins may be somehow linked to her death. We will be reporting more on this bizarre story as it develops. This is Sandra Cummins, WITV News."

Gerald Pence ushered the men to the door. Agent Broyles turned to him.

"Mr. Pence, I wish I could say that this case is closed, but I still worry for you and your daughter while this guy Atkins is on the loose. I'd like to post a guard here until we hear more from George Town."

"That's very kind of you, sir, but I'm sure my daughter and I can take care of ourselves."

He gripped Broyles by the arm and edged him closer to the door. Broyles tried for the last word.

"By the way, Mr. Pence, about this project of yours."

"Project?"

"Your experimental aircraft. I hear that it will be quite revolutionary. Something the government might be interested in."

Gerald chuckled. "Would this be the real reason you want to post a guard here?"

"That's part of it," Broyles returned. "If Atkins is determined enough to get the plans for whatever reason, he might resort to anything including a flyer toward you and your daughter."

Gerald released Broyles's arm and smiled. "Gentlemen, do you all have a minute? I'd like to introduce you to the Altair."

Steve looked over to Doc begging acquiescence. Doc scowled.

"I really think we should head on back . . ."

"Doc, just a minute or two. You should really see this thing," Steve begged.

Sergeant Wilson shrugged. "I'm in no rush, Doc. The copter's not due back south for a couple of more hours."

"Whose side are you on?" Doc barked. "Okay, okay. A couple of minutes and that's all!"

Doc turned the model of the Altair in his hands.

"Fascinating," he said, momentarily forgetting about the trip back south.

"You say this thing will actually fly?" he asked.

Gerald chuckled. "Theoretically, yes. The computer does it all. It wouldn't fly if a human tried to pilot it."

Agent Broyles stood at the drawing table flipping through the blueprints.

"What will this thing do that other aircraft can't?"

Gerald walked over to Broyles. "This is all theory, you understand. But the craft would fly at mach 8—much faster in space where it's capable of going—and is powered by a hydrogen engine. It would have stealth features and would be equipped with laser weapons that could destroy anything in the air today."

Broyles whistled. "My God, any nation that had a fleet of these would rule the skies."

Doc placed the model back on its stand and asked, "How could the human body withstand such speeds and changes in direction?"

Gerald picked up the model and turned it in his hands.

"An environmental correction system adjusts to the outside pressures as the craft does its gyrations, the atmosphere inside the craft normalizes and life goes on as usual," he blithely answered.

"It's all Dutch to me." Broyles shook his head. "When do you expect to put this thing to the test?"

"Gentlemen, I've said it several times now, and I'll say it again. This is all theory."

Gerald began rolling up the blue prints. "We would have to manufacture both the air frame and the hydrogen engine. It would take a special alloy to withstand the heat of high speeds and atmosphere reentry from space. This would be just a few of the technical problems. None of these things are currently available."

He moved to a corner of the room, retrieved a large tube, and slipped the blue prints into it. "Let me assure you, the Altair is a paper dream and nothing more." Gerald placed the tube in the slot of a cabinet on the wall of the den and turned toward the men.

"So Agent Broyles, the government will have a long wait, if indeed it ever comes to pass."

He moved them all toward the exit. "In the meantime, my family needs some privacy. After all, Christmas is almost on us, and we haven't done any decorating or shopping."

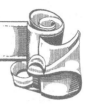

CHAPTER 11

"She must have put up one hell of a fight," the commissioner of police of the Cayman Islands said over the phone. He was reporting back on a conference call to Agent Manning in Chicago and Agent Broyles in Indianapolis.

"There were traces of skin under several of her finger nails, and . . ." He added, in a strong British accent, "I would suspect that if you could get the shirt off of Mr. Atkins, you would see some pretty nasty gouges."

"That might be a problem," Manning said. "We haven't the slightest idea where the hell he is. But if and when we do apprehend him, and his DNA matches the skin samples, we will have him cold."

The Commissioner continued his report. "If that weren't enough, her scuba mask strap was torn as if it had been ripped off her face. It smacks of premeditated murder."

"Incidentally," Manning said, "The funds Atkins deposited in the bank down there will be evidence against Upstein when he goes to trial up here."

"Not to worry, old chap," the commissioner replied, "we've impounded it. As for Atkins, I would suggest you put an all-points out on him. If, as you say, he is intent on procuring the plans for that experimental aircraft, he'll stop at nothing. I would be concerned for the safety of the Pences."

"That we are," Manning responded." Thank you for the info and keep us informed of any further developments."

"Right-o, old chap." They hung up.

"Broyles, are you still on the other line?"

"Yes."

"Any ideas?"

"Not at the moment. But we better start humpin'. I have a feeling we haven't got a whole bunch of time!"

Christmas was just ten days away. Steve Gordon, Jason Bonneau, and Bob Zimmerman sat across the desk from Doc Ewing in the state police headquarters. Steve blew into his coffee cup and looked over the edge toward Doc.

"Any word about when Deputy Bentley will be out of the hospital?"

Doc smiled. "He'll be home for Christmas, thank the Lord." He added, "I sent a couple of the lodge housekeepers over to his house for several days to help the family while he was recuperating. This will be a special Christmas for them . . . and how about you? Have you done all your shopping?"

Steve laughed. "Carolyn does all of that. She buys for the kids, and we've agreed that she gets what she wants for herself and lets me wrap it."

Jason reached over and jostled Steve's shoulder. "How's she comin' along, Steve?"

"She's in some pain, but she'll be all right. She's a real trooper about this thing."

"When does she go in for her tests?"

"Early January, but we're putting all that out of our minds for now," Steve answered. "The boys are home on Christmas break and we're going to make the most of it."

Doc lifted his coffee cup in a toast. "Good for you all! Incidentally, while we're all together, we might want to start thinking about the deer hunt for next fall."

Steve reared back in his chair and shook his head.

"Let's wait 'til after the holidays. I haven't gotten over this one yet."

"Good idea!" Jason injected, and that seemed to be settled.

"By the way, I have an interesting tidbit to tell you guys."

Steve motioned the three heads toward him.

"When Robert came home from Purdue the other day, he told me a very interesting story. He said that our abducted executive, Gerald Pence, was the same guy that Robert's close friend in the aeronautical department was working with on a very hush-hush project."

"What kind of a project?" Doc inquired in an apprehensive tone.

"I'm not sure I understand it all, but Robert said it had something to do with Purdue's Raisbeck engineering program and the development of an experimental fuselage and engine. That's all his friend would say."

"The XSA . . . but Pence told us—"

"I know what he told us." Steve interrupted. "But I think he was trying to get the government guys off his back. From what Bobby inferred, the Altair is much more than a paper dream."

There was a moment of complete silence and thought. Doc leaned across the desk and spoke in a low voice. "Let's put this Pence thing behind us, Steve. It's out of our hands and we've got our own problems here."

Steve sipped his coffee. "Technically, it might all be over, but I just can't get the thought out of my mind that those people up there are still in danger. I just feel like I'm part of it, and I've abandoned ship."

Doc shook his head in frustration. "How many times do I have to tell you it's none of our business? Now, can it, for God's sake!"

Steve sipped again and stared out the office window. He hadn't heard a word Doc Ewing said.

Part Two

THE FLIGHT

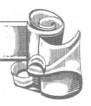

CHAPTER 12

A merican Airlines flight 4081 touched down at Jean Lesage International Airport in Quebec at 10:16 p.m., twenty-three minutes late. It quickly rolled to gate 11 and began discharging its passengers. A bearded man, carrying a briefcase was the last to emerge. He walked immediately to the front of the airport and hailed a cab.

"Le Concorde!" he mumbled and the taxi pulled off.

The small group dispersed from the grave site. Steve Gordon and his two sons, Steven Jr. and Robert, remained, silently staring at Carolyn Pence's grave. The rain spattered on their umbrellas, and Steve shivered, squeezing his coat collar tightly around his neck. It was a cold September morning. At length, Robert placed his hand on his father's shoulder.

"We'll catch pneumonia out here, Dad. I think it's time to go."

Steve nodded and after a slight pause, the three began their walk to the car parked on the roadside. All were silent as they maneuvered the country road toward home. Steven Jr. sat behind the wheel, Steve was in the front seat beside him, and Robert sat in the back, staring absently out at the passing scenery. The drone of the car engine prodded Robert's memories of the past nine months.

His mother, Carolyn, had been diagnosed with breast cancer in early December of last year, and although the doctor had been encouraging in his prognosis, she did not respond to treatment. From the initial diagnosis she had gone into progressive decline. Both he and Steven Jr. volunteered to put their college careers on hold during the crisis, but their father vehemently opposed the idea. Thus, Steve was left with the burden of caregiving, which progressively worsened as the end neared.

Fortunately, through the good graces of Doc Ewing, the state park personnel supervisor, Steve had been given an extended leave of absence from his job as park naturalist. When Steven Jr. and Robert could, they made the trips from Bloomington and West Lafayette respectively, to lend a hand. During summer break, they allowed Steve to fulfill his obligations at the state park while they assumed the duties at home. Then, both Steven Jr. and Robert went back to school in early September, and Steve returned to his leave of absence status.

They turned off of Route 46, wound past Park View Lake and up the hill to the driveway in the front of their house. For minutes they sat silently, each staring at the structure that rolled back memories of years past. Steve fought back a tearful breakdown, thanks to the voice of Steven Jr.

"Let's go in now, Dad? A good log fire is just what we all need."

Steve nodded his head and gave his older son a wholesome slug on his shoulder. They proceeded solemnly into the house. They sat in front of the fireplace watching the crackling blaze as it responded to Robert's new log. He returned to his chair and looked over at his father's expressionless stare.

"Dad, why don't you quit your job at the park and come to West Lafayette? Purdue could use a good forestry professor, and it would put all the memories of this house behind you."

Steve nodded. "I couldn't do that to Doc. We're short of personnel at the park as it is, and that would put a terrible burden on him. Besides, I'm not sure I would qualify for that kind of responsibility."

"Or," Steven Jr. said, "you could come to IU! They've got departments there that could use your experience."

Robert exploded in good humor. "Departments? Hell, they call them prison cells at Purdue!" Steven retorted.

"At Purdue—what they laughingly call a university—I hear that beards are the rage with the girls. Almost all of them have one."

Robert came back.

"I hear the IU library burned down last week, and they lost both books. One wasn't even colored in yet!"

Steven reciprocated. "I know you're from Purdue because I saw your class ring while you were picking your nose!"

Finally Steve intervened. "Okay, okay you guys. That's all. I know you think your lightening things up here, but I'm not in the mood. Besides all your quips are old stuff."

The three reverted their attention back to the fireplace. Robert spoke up. "Think about it, Dad."

Both boys were off to school, and Steve was now suffering the deafening hum of loneliness. Maybe Robert's suggestion had merit. It was morning, and Steve was bolting down a light breakfast when the phone rang. It was Doc.

"Are you watching television?" His voiced was stressed.

"No, why?"

"Turn it on and call me back."

Steve clicked his TV on and stepped back to watch. Both World Trade buildings were on fire. There was chaos in the surrounding streets. There were fire trucks, police cars, and crowds of people running and screaming. Al Jennings, commentator for the network, was nervously explaining the situation.

"There is no question that this is an act of terrorism." His voice cracked. "It has also been reported that the Pentagon in Washington, DC, has been hit with a heavy loss of life."

Steve was aghast. He picked up the phone and dialed Doc's number.

"I will be there as soon as I can."

"There's no rush. We're clear here. But I'm concerned about my son. He's been at the Pentagon for several weeks, and I've heard nothing from him."

They hung up. Steve turned toward the TV.

"Bastards!"

The man with the beard sat in the darkness of suite 311 on the third floor of the hotel Le Concorde in Quebec City. A raspy voice across from him spoke out.

"When did you get the message to come here?"

"Two days ago. I had trouble getting a flight."

"Do you have the package with you?"

The Voice drew on a cigarette, lighting up his face temporarily, but not enough for the bearded man to recognize any features. He reached down for his briefcase and shoved it toward the Voice.

"This is all I have. It was the briefcase that Gerald Pence supposedly had with him the night he was kidnapped."

"The plans?"

"Such as they are." The beard responded sardonically. There was the clicking of opening latches and the rustle of paper. The Voice withdrew a small flashlight and studied the contents of the briefcase behind its raised lid. Shortly the light went out, and the lid slammed shut.

"These are worthless!"

"It was all we could find on the damn thing!" the owner of the beard whined.

He leaned toward the Voice trying to discern the face. There was another draw on the cigarette, but no recognition.

"Who are you?" the beard demanded. There was a pause.

"I wouldn't worry yourself about that. Suffice it to say that we are quite familiar with your relationship with Mr. Pence, his daughter, and I understand, the now deceased Mrs. Pence. That's what made you worth something to us. That's why, Mr. Atkins, you are here now."

Atkins fell back in his chair.

"Okay, you know who I am. Why shouldn't I know who I'm dealing with here . . . And when do I get the money?"

"Money? Money for what? This worthless junk? You were to get us the detailed plans for Pence's magical aircraft. Detailed . . . not comic book sketches."

Atkins jumped to his feet and made a motion toward the Voice.

"Stay where you are, Atkins. Don't come a step closer!"

Atkins hesitated and returned to his seat. He regained his composure.

"As president and CEO of Porter Aviation, you should know what goes into designing and building a standard modern aircraft, and you should have at least a hunch of what it would take to build the kind of craft Pence is allegedly building." The Voice continued. "We need specs on the computer programing, body structure, and formulas for fuel, stealth capabilities . . . formulas, formulas, formulas."

Atkins smirked. "And if you had all that what would you do with it?"

The Voice went silent and then spoke.

"We have access to some of the brightest, most profound minds in the world. With the authentic specifications, we could build this thing."

"Sir, I am not doing one more thing for you or your . . . whatever group you belong to . . . unless, number one, I get paid for what I've already done . . . junk or not, and . . . that if I can, by some miracle, get the kind of specifications you're talking about, I will be compensated with one hell of a lot of money!"

Silence followed. The Voice took a deep pull on his cigarette and then lighted another one from it. Atkins could see more details of the lower face. In the sustained glow, a mustache showed itself and then there was darkness again.

"I think you'd better rethink that, Mr. Atkins. I could pick up the phone right now and turn you in to the Canadian police. You would then be extradited to the authorities in your country and tried for first degree murder. That could mean life in jail . . . or worse."

The Voice continued. "You will be handed an envelope. You are to read its contents and follow its instructions. I would suggest you do so after you leave this hotel."

There was a rustle of movement and the Voice disappeared. It was replaced by the form of a man approaching from a door to the rear of the suite. He handed Atkins a large envelope and then left the room.

A small lamp was turned on, and Atkins found himself alone. In anger, he bolted from the room and out of the hotel onto the dark streets of Quebec City.

Agent Koloski was worried. He had been assigned to keep both Gerald Pence and his daughter under surveillance during the hours of two and eight—the afternoon shift. His instructions were to keep them under observation whether inside or outside their home. It hadn't happened that way since four hours ago. Gerald and Becky had emerged from their garage in their car at three fifteen and were stopped at the foot of the driveway by Koloski.

"It's a matter of your safety," he had said when he informed them that he would accompany them to wherever they wished to go. Gerald exploded.

"Damn it to hell! We're getting sick and tired of you people hounding us night and day. I've told your office that we could take care of ourselves! We don't need protection, and that's what I mean!"

Koloski tried to argue that he was under orders to do so, but in the foulest language he could muster, Gerald threatened that if he followed them, he would face legal action or physical violence—whichever seemed the most appropriate.

Then, in a calmer mood, Gerald assured the agent that they would return within the hour, and with that, sped off. It was now seven fifteen, and the Pences had not returned. He nervously called the main office and explained the situation to his superior.

"Then you might have time to search their house."

"Search their house?" Koloski parroted. I'll bet the place is loaded with security devices," his supervisor responded in a patronizing tone.

"The security system switch is in the closet to the left of the entrance to the house. The code is 3341. You have thirty seconds to disable it."

"How the hell do you know all that?" Koloski screamed.

"Why Agent Koloski, we are the FBI. We know everything. Now get busy!"

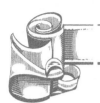

CHAPTER 13

Gerald turned off of Payne Road and into the Crooked Creek Apartment complex.

"Isn't this where . . ." Becky started.

"Janet Taylor lives. Yes, she's going with us."

Becky smiled. "The real thing, eh?"

"The real thing!"

Janet came out of her apartment building, bag in hand, and climbed into the back seat. She leaned between the two in the front.

"Where to, Boss?"

They weaved through northwest Indianapolis onto Interstate 65 and finally onto Route 52 north, toward West Lafayette. They traveled awhile in silence.

"Why do I feel like such a fugitive?" Becky moaned.

Gerald chuckled. "Because I guess we are at this point. Those federal guys are no more interested in our safety than they are in a can of bean soup. They've gotten caught up in the mystery of my project, and that's the only reason they've been hounding us."

"That's what frightens me, Dad. What will they do? Your effort to sidetrack them hasn't worked. They think this whole thing is real."

"Now you're doubting me?"

"No, no, but I haven't seen anything yet. How real is all this?"

"You'll see soon, my dear daughter. Very soon."

Gerald was hoping to reach their destination before dark. They were forty-five minutes away. They just might make it. They returned to silence. They turned left at Monroe toward Stockton, and from there to a dirt road heading north. They traveled for two-and-a-half miles before turning into a gated farm entrance. Gerald reached for an opener on his sun visor and pushed the button. The gate slid open, and they proceeded down the roadway, closing the gate behind them. They approached a small, two story frame house on a hill to the right and a large barn to the left. Gerald drove up the driveway leading to the house.

"Who lives here?" Becky asked.

"Old friends. Janet and I have visited here several times. You'll like them. You better . . . This is where we're staying for a while."

It was now dark.

Agent Koloski walked cautiously up the driveway toward the Pence house. At the door, he peered in the left side window. There was a night light inside, and he had a limited view of the interior. He could make out a large picture window in the rear of the great room, but that was the extent of his perusal. He studied the door lock and determined that it was pickable. From a small felt packet he removed the instrument he needed and began probing. There was a click. He turned the knob and opened the door. The alarm warning system began beeping. He rushed to the closet to the left of the door and with flash light in hand found the control box. 3341 . . . and the beeping stopped. He was free to roam. Into the great room. Nothing. He moved down the back hall leading to a door at the far end. It was locked. He spied the service chest against the wall, and on a hunch, began searching it. He found a key. It fit the lock. He turned it.

He never heard the explosion.

Two fire trucks and an ambulance kept FBI Agent Kyle Broyle's car from coming all the way up the driveway. The Pence house was a disaster. The fire had pretty well gone out and just the haze of the after-smoke hung over the area. Koloski lay on a gurney beside the ambulance, being attended to by several paramedics. One spoke to Broyles, shaking his head in amazement.

"I don't see how this guy survived the blast. Apparently, the door he was trying to open pushed him far enough away from the core of the explosion that it saved his life."

Broyles bent over the conscious Koloski.

"You're a lucky guy, Koloski. Not even a broken bone. What happened in there?"

Agent Koloski's throat was dry, and he painfully rasped an answer.

"Beats the hell out of me. I can't remember much after I turned the alarm off. I remember finding a key and I think . . ." Koloski coughed violently for a moment. "I think I got it in the lock and apparently that set something off."

Broyles pulled out his cell phone and dialed a number as another FBI agent approached him. Broyles waved him off as he waited for an answer. An answering machine fielded his call:

"Agent Charles Manning is out of the office or is busy on another line. At the tone, please leave your name, a number where you can be reached, and a brief message."

"Manning, this is Broyles. Call me when you can." He clicked off. He turned to the other agent. "This puts a different light on this whole business. Hence forth, Mr. Gerald Pence is a felon on the loose!"

Dan Upstein, former executive vice president of the now-defunct Pence Technology Corporation, stood trial in an Indianapolis court on counts of embezzlement and laundering, kidnapping, and aiding and abetting at least one murder and probably another. Ralph Berman was rated one of the best defense attorneys in Indiana, but try as he may, with every defense known to a clever lawyer, he could not sway the court from the fact that Upstein was guilty as hell. As it was, he was able to modify the murder allegations on the basis of ambiguous evidence. Nevertheless, Upstein was found guilty of the other charges and sentenced to a total of forty years in prison. Berman assured Upstein that he would submit an appeal, which he did shortly afterward. In the meantime, Dan Upstein entered the Indiana state prison to begin what might be a lifetime of incarceration, pending the outcome of the appeal.

Homer and Anna Cummings were hosts to Gerald, Becky, and Janet in the old two-story farm house twelve-and-a-half miles south of West Lafayette. They all sipped

118

hot chocolate as they sat before a warm fire in the living room, digesting a lavish country supper.

Homer and Anna appeared to be typical Hoosier country folk. Homer was tall, lean, and tan. He bore a sparkle in his eyes and what seemed to be a perpetual smile on his face. His hair was thinning and graying at the temples, but his build was muscular, reflecting many years of manual labor. Anna was short and rather stout. She was born in Germany and came to the states at the age of fourteen. She became a citizen seven years later. Although she spent many hours in her kitchen, her face was tan and creased from her many years of outdoor exposure. Her face nevertheless expressed kindness and compassion.

The appearances, however, were an illusion. The couple were actually tenants hired by a covert group from Purdue to guard the area from intruders, and they were very serious about their jobs.

"Farmer Campbell up the way regularly comes back and forth on the road, but that's pretty much all the traffic we've had fer quite a piece, 'cept fer the crew's comin' and goin'," Homer informed Gerald, referring to the dirt road in front of the farm.

Becky was bewildered. "Crew? What are we talking about?" She looked toward Janet.

"Janet, do you know what's going on here?" Janet smiled and gestured toward Gerald. "That's for your Dad to say."

Gerald looked over at Homer. "I think the fire needs feeding. Mind if I put another log on?"

"Be my guest."

Gerald picked up a small log next to the stone fireplace and fed it into the dwindling fire. He stopped in front of Becky. "Patience, my darling daughter. Patience." He resumed his seat and sipped his hot chocolate.

"Are you three stayin' awhile?" Anna asked after some silence.

"I'm afraid we're going to be nuisances for quite some time." He glanced at his watch. "By now, this is the only home we have."

Becky was startled. "What do you mean, Dad?"

"You remember we agreed that we were not returning to Indianapolis," he responded.

"Well . . . yes, but what about the house? Are we not putting it up for sale?"

"If my timing is right, there's nothing left to sell. Before we left, I placed an explosive inside the lab beside the main frame. It was due to go off at seven forty-five."

"But why?" Becky pleaded.

"Becky. The main frame could not be moved without alerting the guys outside the house. It contained too much data about the project. It had to be destroyed."

"But Dad, what if someone was in there when it went?"

"Then I'd say I was in a heap of trouble!"

Doc Ewing's son was indeed at the Pentagon when the terrorists hit it, but on the far side of the building from the impact area. He had received an official commendation for his part in the rescue efforts. He was a chip off the old block.

September through November was the busiest time of the year for the park, and it kept Steve's mind off his tragic loss. From morning until closing time at six in the evening, the park was constantly full of visitors admiring the blazing color the Indiana fall. Steve's three nature center classes were constantly at capacity, which meant that he would be staying late into the evening with his regular administrative duties. He dreaded the thought of going home.

It was comfortably warm as he stood on the rear deck of his house. The moon was full as he stared over the trees to the glimmering lake below. How many times had he and Carolyn stood there and admired such an evening of beauty. It brought back the aroma of her perfume, the softness of her body as they sat on the deck bench, holding hands, sipping wine, and talking of nothing important. He hung his head. How many pervasive memories will haunt him until he can cope with her death?

The phone rang.

"High, Dad!" It was Robert. "How are things with you down there in the jungle?"

"Passive. How many tests have you flunked this week?"

"None so far. In fact, I got an A on a Calculus test yesterday."

"God, you mean you understand that stuff."

Robert laughed. "Sometimes. It depends on the problem."

He got serious. "Dad, have you thought any more about coming up here?"

"Frankly, no. This is a busy time down here and I really haven't had time to think about anything else. Besides, Robert . . . what happens when you graduate, and I'm up there away from everyone?"

"That's two years away, Pops, and anyway, I'll probably land a job up here."

"Doing what?"

"Oh, there's a bundle of opportunities for employment. Come up and take your pick." He laughed.

They chatted for another few minutes and hung up. Steve stared blankly at the cradled phone. Yes, he had given thought to getting away from this house. To getting away from thinking he heard her calling him. To walking from one empty room to another. To waking up from the recurring dreams of searching for her down empty streets and asking faceless people if they knew where she was. He wanted to get away, but he also had to think of Steven, at IU. So staying put in Williams Creek for now was his only recourse.

CHAPTER 14

Daryl Atkins walked into a small pub two blocks down from the Le Concorde. He ordered a beer and sat down in a booth to read the letter he had been given at the hotel. His hands shook as he tore open the envelope. To his surprise, it contained five American one-thousand-dollar bills and a note. Partial pay at least, he thought. He read the note.

> Mr. Atkins,
>
> Given that your relationship with the Pence family is highly dubious at best, you at least have a connection. Since it is obvious that recent events have shown Gerald Pence to be a rather indomitable person, we do not expect him to freely cooperate with us in passing on what we need to know about this special aircraft of his. His daughter in our hands, however, might loosen his tongue. If you can accomplish this, it will be worth fifty thousand dollars to you. We will follow your progress.
>
> Good Luck.

Good God, he thought. How in the hell do they think I'm going to pull that off? He swigged his beer, and reread the note. Trying to abduct Pence's daughter would be walking into a hornet's nest. I couldn't get within ten feet of her, let alone get by her father. Fifty thousand was not enough to take that kind of risk.

He finished his beer and left the pub. He walked back the way he had come and stood in front of the entrance to the Le Concorde. He had to talk to the Voice, get some clarification, and barter for more than fifty thousand. The doorman approached him.

"Are you in need of assistance, sir?"

"Yes! Is it possible to have a note delivered to a friend in suite 311?"

"Certainly, sir," was the response.

"I'll write it out in the lobby."

He brushed past the doorman and sat down at a table. He began writing. Then he stopped in midsentence. A thought occurred to him. He balled the note up, jammed it into his coat pocket and walked back onto the street. He slipped the doorman a twenty dollar bill.

"Thanks anyway."

He hailed a cab.

Atkins purchased a cell phone at an all-night convenience store several blocks from the hotel, along with the mandatory one month of calls. He then checked into a flophouse near the bay. It was now one forty-five in the morning, and he dropped onto the bed in total exhaustion. He fell into a deep sleep, street clothes and all.

They had retired for the night in the farm house. Much to Becky's chagrin, Janet had gone with her father to a separate bedroom. Yes, this was the real thing, and as much as she liked Janet, she found it difficult to accept the fact that she was replacing her mother in her father's heart. She could not sleep. She stared at a shadowed ceiling and wondered about the evening events. Who were the crews? Why did her father destroy the mainframe computer the way he did? Who were these simple farm people? What the hell was going on here?

She had asked her father all of these questions and his answer was to wait until morning. Then, as she began drifting off, she thought of Steve Gordon's visit to their house earlier in the year. He was quite an impressive man, and she had thought of him many times since. She finally fell asleep.

Ever since his mother's death, Steven Jr, found it difficult to concentrate on his studies. Maybe it was not so much her loss that bothered him, but the effect it was having on his father. His father's normally happy outlook on life had turned sullen. It was getting to be more of an ordeal to talk to him. He walked out of his chemistry class and stared at his D-minus test paper. Last year he had achieved a 3.8 grade average, and a D-minus in one of his best subjects would not do.

He walked over to the Pi Beta Phi sorority house and paged Jessica, a close friend. He had to talk to someone. They sipped cokes at the student union lounge. Jessica was a sophomore from Portage, Indiana, majoring in biology.

She was petite, whereas Steven was tall and lanky. They had been dating since she arrived at IU the previous year and were known among their friends as the "cute couple."

"I'm thinking of sitting out a semester, Jess."

She took a swallow of her drink and nodded her head. "It might be for the best, Steve. You've been distracted ever since your mom died."

"It's Dad. It's hit him worse than Robert and me. When he's not at the park, he mopes around the house. He's not eating regularly, and I don't think he gets much sleep. If I were there for him, I could ride herd until he gets a hold of himself."

She took his hand. "I'd miss you."

"Hey, William's Creek is only a half-hour trip from here. You could come over on weekends and work at the park in the summer. They'd welcome your biology background."

"I'll think on that."

"It's early enough in the semester that it won't hurt my grades if I drop out now."

Jessica smiled and leaned toward Steven. "If you really think it's the right thing to do, then do it."

"Yeah, now all I have to do is sell Dad on the idea."

David Berman's appeal on behalf of Dan Upstein was denied. After a short conference with Upstein at the state prison, he went back to the drawing board.

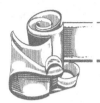

CHAPTER 15

Boat traffic on the bay woke Atkins nine hours later. He splashed water on his face from the sink in his room, picked up his cell phone, and dialed a number. It rang twice.

"Carl, this Daryl."

"Goddamn, where the hell have you been? Things have pretty much gone to hell since you've been gone."

"Look Carl, I don't have much time to talk. I need you to do me a favor."

"Name it!" he answered.

"You're familiar with Gerald Pence and his technical gang."

"Sure am."

"I'm going to give you their home address in Indianapolis, and I want you to go down there and check it out for me."

There was a pause on the other end of the line. Then . . .

"Whatever for?"

"Never mind that. I need to know who goes in and who comes out and at what times. Pay particular attention to the Pence girl."

"This sounds very peculiar, Daryl. What the hell are you up to?"

"It'll be worth one thousand dollars to you if you don't ask questions and do as I ask."

Another pause. "Okay. When do you need all this?"

"Right away. Now please, Carl, time is of the essence."

"Where can I reach you?"

"I'll call you in four days. That should be enough time for you . . . and Carl . . . for God's sake don't tell anyone you talked to me or about what I've asked you to do."

Atkins hung up. He realized that he hadn't eaten since yesterday noon. He paid his bill, hailed another taxi and directed it to the Quebec City airport. He would grab a sandwich there.

Agent Manning returned the call from Broyles in Indianapolis.

"What's up, Kyle?"

"Not a whole lot . . . What's down? Gerald Pence pulled one on us. He blew up his house two nights ago."

"He what?"

"He apparently set a time bomb in his laboratory and blew the whole area to hell including the damn mainframe. He and his daughter skedaddled several hours before it went off."

"Where the hell was our surveillance?"

"They faked him out. Took off in their car . . . told him they'd be back in an hour."

"Dumb son of a bitch!"

"He's lucky to be alive. He was in the house when it blew."

"Jesus, Kyle, it sounds like we've lost complete control!"

"Not entirely, Chuck. We're taking a look at the son of that naturalist guy from the state park in Williams Creek."

"Steve Gordon? What does he have to do with all this now?"

"His son, Robert, is involved with the Raisbeck Engineering Department at Purdue."

"So?"

"The department specializes in exotic new aeronautical designs, as I understand it, and rumor has it that they're working on a highly classified project."

"You think there's a connection then."

"It's worth looking into. I'm going up to meet with our people in West Lafayette on Wednesday to see what they know about it."

"Be careful, Kyle. Let's not let any cats out of the bag."

"I'll get back to you when I return."

Manning slowly cradled the phone and lit a cigarette . . . a habit he had recently developed. He took a drag and blew smoke toward the ceiling. He didn't like the way things were going.

After a hearty breakfast, Gerald, Becky, and Janet descended the basement stairs of the farmhouse. They moved near a large bookcase against the wall on the far side of the room. Gerald carefully slid it aside to reveal a steel door. He lifted a latch and pulled it open. He motioned for the two girls to follow him into a dimly lit tunnel. They traveled for what Becky estimated to be the length of a football field and came to another steel door. This one had a coded security lock. Gerald pushed buttons four times. There was an audible click, and he opened the door. They entered a huge room, and what Becky saw took her breath away. On a large platform in front of them stood the daunting fuselage of the Altair.

"My God!" Becky cried out. "It's real. "She turned to Gerald. "Is it ready to fly?"

"Not quite," he said. "It's undergoing data transfer from the mainframe computer over there."

He pointed to the wall at their left, where the massive computer sat with a large cable running from it to the craft.

"It will take some time for the main system and the two backups to process over to the aircraft before she's ready for testing."

Becky perused the rest of the room. There were benches on all sides filled with electronic and other technical equipment. To the right of where they were standing were three large windows revealing another room filled with even more equipment. There were four men in white smocks—two monitoring a panel below the main frame, one inspecting the underside of the aircraft, and the fourth meandering over to where they stood.

"Good morning, Mr. Pence. How can we help you?"

"Good morning, Jake. May I introduce my daughter, Becky, and of course you know Ms. Taylor."

He politely nodded his head.

"How are things progressing?" Gerald asked.

"Couldn't be better," Jake responded.

"I notice there are only four of you here. Aren't there more on the team?"

"Oh yes," was the answer, "the other four are in classes at the university this morning. They'll be here this afternoon."

Gerald asked for the list of team names, and Jake retrieved a clipboard from one of the desks. After a close scrutiny Gerald looked up.

"There's nine names here."

"Yes, sir. An Indian boy has joined the flock. Real adept in electronics."

"Indian? Muslim? How much do you know about him?"

"He checks out, sir. He has a magnificent record at school. He and his parents are now citizens . . . And, sir, I'm not sure he's Muslim by faith."

"When he comes in, I want to talk to him."

"Yes, sir."

Gerald motioned for the two women to follow him to the base of the aircraft. There were steps leading to the interior. They climbed them into a cabin of deceptive simplicity. There were two seats behind a control board of dials and LCDs. The apparent pilot's seat was to the left, the copilot is to the right, as is the case in standard aircraft. Behind them were six seats, and in the rear was what appeared to be a supply cabinet.

"Tell me about all this," Becky remarked.

Gerald smiled and motioned for the two women to be seated behind the pilot's compartment.

"Now, my children, I shall tell you the story of a magnificent aircraft.

It will fly anywhere on this earth at a speed of . . . in your language . . . six thousand, eighty-eight miles per hour at full power, three thousand, eight hundred and five at cruising speed. At that speed, it will fly coast to coast in thirty-nine minutes and around the world in a little over two hours. Think what it would do at maximum speed.

It has stealth capabilities, and it is armed with lasers that will knock anything out of the air that exists today. It can fly into and sustain itself in space indefinitely, depending on the supply of food and water."

Becky said, "You say it flies solely by computer?"

"That's correct. It's controlled by the voice of the pilots."

"You mentioned backups."

"There are two. If the main computer should quit, the second takes over while the third repairs the first."

"Can anyone fly this thing?"

"By handprint ID only." Gerald walked to the control panel.

"These two LCDs on the right and left of the panel will identify the pilots. If they are strange hands, the ship will not respond."

There was a moment of quiet reflection. Becky spoke up.

"But, you don't know if all of this will work, do you, Dad?"

"I'm sure of all my mathematical formulas. We'll run ground tests when the data transfer is completed, and then . . ."

"The flight!" Becky said.

"The flight!" Gerald repeated.

Gerald studied the list of the project crew and looked across at the Indian boy. They were sitting at a table in the adjoining room.

"Farid Sherazi is not an Indian name."

The youth shifted in his chair. He was of average height, light skinned and black hair. He wore a mustache and goatee. With a large hooked nose, he looked every bit like a person from the Middle East.

"No, Sir. It is Iranian. I was born there. My parents and I ran off to India to escape the oppression of the Iranian government. We came to the United States five years ago."

"Are you now naturalized citizens?"

Farid leaned back proudly. "As of a month ago!"

"Congratulations."

Gerald shuffled some papers on the desk, picked one up and studied it. He looked up at the student.

"I hope you understand that with world events as they are, I can't be too careful with the security of this project."

"Yes, sir, I understand that.

Gerald rose and crossed the room to a rack of documents. He pulled out a thick notebook and returned to the table.

"I hear that you are quite good at electronics."

"That's my minor, sir."

He handed Farid the notebook. "In there you will find the formulas that I think prove the validity of this program. I want you to study them and tell me what you think."

"Yes, sir."

They both rose and moved to the door. "And, Farid . . . no copies."

"I understand, sir."

Airport security was almost unbearable since the tragedy of 9-11. It was doubly so with Daryl Atkins because he had no baggage. They took him to a special room and questioned him. He identified himself as Spencer Albright, and he had the forged documents to prove it. After a harrowing twenty-five minutes of interrogation, they released him. He boarded United Airlines flight 3819 to Louisville, Kentucky. After a two-and-a-half-hour layover in Newark, Atkins arrived in Louisville at eleven thirty that night. Still under the name of Albright, he rented a car and drove to Greenwood, where he checked into a motel. In his room, he dialed a number on his cell phone. It rang five times and gave in to an answering machine. Carl identified himself and asked for a number to return the call by.

"Carl, this is Daryl. I thought I'd call to see how you were doing on my request. Call me on my cell phone: 817-555-5377. He hung up and went to bed. His cell phone buzzed two hours later.

"I'm glad you called, Daryl. That address you gave me no longer exists."

"What do you mean?"

"It's burned to the ground, and there was no one around to tell me what happened."

"Are you sure you have the right address?"

"Positive!"

"No sign of either of the Pences?"

"None."

"Can you hang around up there and try to find out what happened and where the Pences are?"

"I'll try, Daryl, but I can't stay long. They're expecting me back in Chicago the day after tomorrow."

Atkins paused for a moment. "On second thought, you've done all you can, Carl. Go on back to Chicago. You'd just be spinning your wheels here in Indianapolis. I'll send you a check."

"Just a couple of hundred, Daryl. To cover expenses." He clicked off.

What now? he wondered. He wouldn't be able to sleep so he turned television on and sat down to think things out.

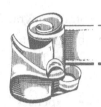

CHAPTER 16

October was dissolving into November, and traffic at the park was dropping off. Steve's nature lectures were cut to one a day, and that was in the afternoon. Thus he had more time for his other responsibilities and could leave the center at a more decent hour in the evening. Steven Jr had taken a semester off to spend more time with his dad, and although, admittedly, this had made the grieving period from Carolyn's death more bearable, he had argued emphatically against the idea. But Steven had stood his ground and capped the discussion with the fact that he had already done the deed. Steve pouted for a day afterward but resigned himself to the situation. Besides, it was nice to come home to a clean house and hot meals.

They sat out on the deck sipping their coffee after dinner, and Steven suddenly came forward with the idea of the two of them traveling north to pay a visit to his brother, Robert. Things were slowing down at the park, Steven had said, and it would do his father good to get away. Besides, he would like to see if all those terrible things he'd been saying about Purdue were true.

"Doc's son, Jon, is coming in tomorrow to say goodbye. He's being shipped off with his unit to Afghanistan next week. I've been invited to lunch with them, and I'll see if Doc can spare me for a couple of days."

They had eaten lightly at the lodge, and Doc bravely bid Jon a bon voyage knowing that it might be the last time he would see him. Steve realized that his supervisor was deep in thought as they remained at the dining table with their coffee. Perhaps this was not the time to bring Steven's suggestion up, but after a while he did.

"There's no ulterior motive here is there, Steve?"

"Ulterior motive? Not that I know of. Why do you say that?"

"Last December you mentioned Robert's conversation concerning a special project going on in the aeronautical department of Purdue. That's still not on your mind is it?"

"The Pence thing? Haven't given it a thought, Doc."

Steve was cleared to go for the week.

"What brings you up this way?" Agent Harold Holtz asked Broyles as they sat across the desk from each other.

"Mind if I smoke?" Broyles asked.

"No, go ahead. I'll join you."

They both lit up.

"Has your office had any dealings with the Raisbeck engineering program in the School of Aeronautics at Purdue?"

Holtz dragged on his cigarette, and exhaled a cloud of smoke over his shoulder. "Why do you ask?"

Broyles opened his briefcase, withdrew a file folder, and slid it across to Hal. Holtz placed his cigarette in an ashtray and began leafing through the folder. Harold was a small slender man in his midfifties. He had been with the FBI for twenty-two years, with an impeccable record of service. He was known for his ability to ferret out inconspicuous but pertinent details in each of the cases assigned to him.

He studied the papers in front of him. "This Pence Corporation thing is familiar to us. Gerald Pence lost his wife in the Cayman Islands, I understand."

"The evidence we have says that she was murdered by Daryl Atkins."

"Now on the loose!"

"Sounds like you're pretty much up to speed on this one."

He retrieved his cigarette, took a puff and crushed it in the ashtray. "To a certain extent. What does that have to do with Purdue?"

Broyles spent the next twenty minutes explaining the details of the case, bringing Holtz up to his reason for his being in West Lafayette.

"You apparently give some credence to this super aircraft of Pence's."

"We saw blueprints, a model, the bank of computers. It all looked quite convincing. Pence claims it's just a pipe dream, but there are too many other parties interested in it to ignore its validity."

"And Raisbeck Engineering is involved?"

"Might be."

Broyles took back his file as Holtz turned to the Mac on his desk. He pecked at the keyboard for a few minutes and pressed the print key. The printer began to clatter as he turned back to Broyles.

"What you say is very interesting, and we might have something for you. A long shot maybe, but . . ." He reached back and pulled the paper from the printer tray.

"There happens to be an old farmer that lives not far from here, complaining to our local police about unusual traffic on the road where he lives. He says it routinely happens in the morning and evening and has been for over a year. He says the vehicles don't come and go all at once, but piecemeal, as if they were timed."

"Where is this on the map?" Broyles asked.

Holtz pulled a wall map down behind him and pointed to an area about twelve miles from where they were.

"It's not on this map, but it's an old dirt road about three miles east of Westpoint, off State Road 28. There are several farms there, but not enough of them to warrant that much traffic."

He walked back to his desk and handed Broyles the copy of the complaint. "It could have nothing to do with what we've been talking about, but it may be worth looking into."

Broyles placed his file folder back in his briefcase and stood up.

"You have time to go out there with me?"

"Actually, I'm due at a meeting in ten minutes, but I'll give you a map." He glanced at his watch. "It's almost five o'clock. You might catch the traffic this guy's complaining about."

Atkins cautiously looked around him. He was certain he had not been followed. He walked slowly up the driveway leading to the Pence house and stood in front of its burnt-out remains. It hadn't seemed that long ago that he had driven up in his Volvo and stood admiring the magnificence of the house. It was his first visit with Gerald and Darlene Pence. He had been invited in with enthusiasm by Gerald. They served drinks and sat down in the massive great room to discuss the reason for his visit. Gerald's wife, Darlene, had obviously been drinking ahead of time, but she was still gracious and friendly, and almost beautiful. He recalled the portrait of her above the fireplace. At the time it was painted, she was radiant and fully beautiful. It was apparent that things had changed, but she was still attractive nevertheless. By her actions that evening he sensed that she would be the lever in dealing with Gerald.

They discussed the sale of Pence Technological Corporation. Three firms were interested in buying, but Atkins felt confident that he would ultimately get the nod.

"I understand that you are working on the design of a state-of-the-art aircraft." Atkins said casually. "We at Porter Aviation are hopeful that the design would be part of the purchase."

Gerald laughed. "All speculative, Daryl. Right now there are only rough sketches and a dream."

"Would you be willing to let us in on the dream?"

By this time, Darlene had had too much to drink and she was getting aggressive. "Our little boy would love to let you play with his little toy!" she slurred. She had then spilled what was left of her drink and went for another one. Gerald had done his best to smooth the situation over, but it was more than obvious that Darlene was an alcoholic.

Atkins recalled meeting Becky when she had come home that evening. She too was attractive, but not beautiful like her mother. She was as gracious as her father when she was introduced to Daryl, but declined a drink, and, after observing the condition of her mother, ushered her out of the room. The meeting had gone on for another hour with nothing much accomplished, and Atkins returned to Chicago.

He walked closer to the debris and picked up a charred part of the window frame that once had adorned the entry way. There were many more visits to Indianapolis, and not all them to see Gerald. He couldn't remember when it was that he and Darlene first slept together. It obviously was when both Gerald and Becky were not at home. He did remember that, at the time, she was terribly drunk. It was when they came to Chicago in the fall of last year that Gerald began to suspect something, and at that point things began going downhill.

Atkins hung his head. Then there was the situation with Dan Upstein, Pence Technology Corporation vice president of operations. In desperation, he had agreed to become an accomplice to Upstein's embezzlement of computer parts in return for the plans that existed for the experimental aircraft. There had been several trips to the Cayman Islands to deposit monies from Upstein's bootlegging. This had all led to total disaster—the failed kidnapping of Gerald Pence, the death of Bill Chenowith, his murder of Darlene in the Caymans, and ultimately the arrest of Upstein.

He returned to the rented car parked on the road side at the bottom of the driveway. He got in and sat thinking. All the money he had banked in the Caymans under the name of Harold Hopkins, the name Upstein told him to use, was by now in a private bank in Bern, Switzerland. That account, amounting to several million dollars, was, however, not under that name any longer. Atkins had taken out a small amount as per his agreement with Upstein, but he could have taken it all. It was now under the name of Daryl H. Atkins.

With a grin on his face, he started the engine and drove off. He hit Interstate 465 at 116th Street and merged toward Chicago.

His mind drifted back to the Caymans. He had called for a boat to take him off the island after he had disposed of Darlene.

"The boat will come from here," he was told, "but it will take a seaplane out of Cienfuegos, Cuba, to get you to the Keys. It'll meet you an hour or so out of Spanish Bay." That part all had gone smoothly.

His cell phone buzzed. He picked it up and flipped it open. "Hello, Mr. Atkins. How are things going?"
He almost drove off the road. It was the Voice.

Farid Sherazi sat across from Gerald in the side room of the underground laboratory. He was confused.

"Mr. Pence, I don't understand how this formula you gave me to study relates to the aircraft. It appears to be the formula for the quantum field theory."

Gerald laughed as he took back the notebook. "I must have given you the wrong book, but in fact, it does partly pertain to the Altair system. In any case, I'm impressed that you recognized what the formula was and that you are so deeply familiar with complicated formulas." Gerald moved to the shelf behind him, replaced the old book, and pulled out a thicker notebook. He returned to the table.

"This book contains most all pertinent formulas for the Altair. I want you to study it carefully. I must have another person who understands the concept completely."

Farid scanned the pages and looked up. "I am honored for your trust."

"Timing is very important here. Can you do this in three days?"

Farid flipped through the notebook again. "Give me just two days."

Purdue's football game that weekend was in East Lansing against Michigan State, so Steve and Steven had no problem getting a room at the Union Club Hotel on the Purdue campus. Robert had been off campus on a special assignment Friday afternoon when they had arrived, so they spent the evening at the union bowling alley and browsing the art gallery. They met Robert for breakfast the following morning at the Sagamore Restaurant.

"Why didn't you guys let me know you were coming?" He complained.

Steve swallowed a bite of toast and smiled. "We always thought you liked surprises."

They chatted while they finished their breakfast and then left the union building for a leisurely walk through the campus. The day was sunny and unseasonably warm for mid-November, so there was a large gathering of students basking on the walls of Academy Park. They went through the Purdue Mall on to Northwestern Avenue.

"Aren't we going in the opposite direction of the ag building?" Steve asked.

"Oh, yes, Dad. I forgot to tell you. I changed my major. I'm now in aeronautical engineering."

Steve barricaded his sons with his arms, and they came to a stop. "When the hell did this happen?"

"Last fall. I got interested in a project that one of my roommates was involved in. After some long conversations about it, I decided it was the field for me."

They continued on. The Bell Tower began chiming 'Hail to Old Purdue' as they approached the Neil Armstrong Hall of Engineering.

"Okay, I'll grant you there's probably more of a future here than agriculture, but damn it, guys, I'm paying the bills, and I think I'm entitled to some consultation before you make these decisions."

The boys nodded passively, and they entered the building.

With an area of approximately two hundred thousand square feet, the Neil Armstrong Hall of Engineering houses the School of Aeronautics and Astronautics, the School of Materials Engineering, and the first School of Engineering Education in the country. The hall's soaring atrium highlighted a display of significant Purdue engineering achievements.

Both Steve and Steven Jr. were in awe as they stood looking up at the glare of the sun shining through the atrium roof. Yes, this was the future, thought Steve, but, oh well, what the hell!

The three of them moved to the basement of the building. After leaving the elevator, they walked down a long hallway. Steve spoke up. "Last December, you mentioned something about a special project that involved some very classified aeronautical experiments with some group here at Purdue. Are you part of that?"

"Raisbeck!" Robert responded proudly. "Yeah, Dad, I am, and there's something I want to show you guys. You, Dad, were very much a part of the situation down at the state park, and again in Indianapolis last fall." He stopped at a door toward the end of the hallway. He pulled out his cell phone, dialed a number, and when there was no answer and no one to let them in, he pushed a code box four times.

"Because of your past involvement, I don't think I'll be betraying any confidences by what you're about to see."

The door opened, and they walked into a large room that appeared to be a chemistry lab. There were two large counters to the left containing chemical flasks, test tubes, and decanters. To the right there was a large blackboard covered with mathematical formulas. Directly in front of them was a drawn curtain on a circular rail. Robert directed them toward the curtain and drew it back. Steve froze for a moment and then approached the pedestal that held the model. He looked at Steven and then back at the model.

"Steven, let me introduce you to the 'Altair.'"

Atkins pulled in to the rest plaza outside of Lebanon. "Things aren't going very well," he informed the Voice. There was a pause.

"We are very much aware of the destruction to Pence's house. We also know that the police are hunting Pence now."

There was another pause while Atkins organized his thoughts. "I notice that your call is originating in the states. You've moved!"

"Very observant, Mr. Atkins. Where are you now?"

"I'm in a rest station on I-65 near Lebanon. I'm surprised you didn't know that."

The Voice ignored the comment. "We have reason to believe that Pence and his daughter are in the West Lafayette area. That means that his project is there too. We also understand that the naturalist from the Williams Creek State Park has a son that might be involved."

"Steve something. God, I thought we were finished with him."

"We might be, but not to worry. Your mission is to get all the detailed data concerning the project. I suggest you start by heading west from where you are. Nose around. Find out what you can."

"Will you be at the same number?"

"No! I'll call you periodically. In any case don't do anything foolish."

The Voice clicked off. Atkins sat for a few minutes thinking over his next move. He then went to the rest room, returned, and got back onto I-65 toward West Lafayette. He had no idea what he was going to do next.

CHAPTER 17

Hal Holtz's meeting was short, and as he sat down at his desk, the phone rang. It was Broyles calling from his cell phone.

"I'm down on this road you directed me to and let me tell you, there are some weird things going on. There are three farms here. One of them is gated, and I watched several cars leaving as I approached. The gate opens and closes automatically . . . pretty technical for an old farm site. But what concerns me is another car ahead of me that paused in front of the gate, took off, came back in the opposite direction, and paused at the gate again. When he saw me, he drove off. What do you make of it?"

Hal grunted and then chuckled. "I can't believe the coincidences here. First you come inquiring about a mysterious project involving Purdue. Then I'm called into a meeting pertaining to that very subject."

"So?"

"Another element has reared its ugly head. The CIA has entered the picture!"

There was a pause on the other end.

"The CIA?!" Broyles scoffed.

"Yeah, and I'll bet dollars to donuts that's the other car you saw."

"Are you going to be there for a while?"

"I can be. Come on back and we'll talk."

They sat in the farmhouse parlor. Gerald was the first to speak.

"I'm not surprised to see you, Steve, since your son Robert here is involved in the project. I'm sorry to hear about your wife."

Steve nodded his head in response. He looked over at Becky. They exchanged smiles. "I'm glad to see both of you again, although I'm just a little bewildered at Robert's part in all this."

"He's been an important contributor," Gerald responded.

Robert's face brightened. "Not as much as I'd like to be. I'm new to this aeronautical technology, so I've got a lot to learn."

Steven Jr. spoke up eagerly. "When are we going to see the real thing?"

Steve hushed him. "I'm sure Mr. Pence is not anxious to involve too many outsiders in his project."

"No, no. I don't consider you outsiders, unless you're secret FBI agents." They all laughed.

"We're almost finished with our data transfer, and I'm due to supervise the disconnect in about half an hour. You can come with me and I'll show you some pretty amazing things."

Homer Cummings stood at a bedroom window facing the dirt road in front of the farm. With his binoculars he followed a slow moving vehicle. It slowed in front of the gate and then stopped for a full two minutes. As it pulled off another car from the opposite direction approached. It slowed as the first car passed it and also stopped in front of the gate. Homer pulled out his cell phone and pressed the redial button.

The group stopped at the head of the basement steps when Gerald's cell phone buzzed. He flipped it open and listened.

"Okay, I'll be right up." He closed the phone and turned to the group. "I've got to leave you for a moment. I'll be right back."

"I think somethin' is goin' on, Mr. Pence. Them cars out there are a might curious about this here place." Homer was visibly concerned.

Gerald looked through the binoculars and watched the second car pull slowly off. He thought for a moment. "Whoever they are, they must have followed the Gordons."

Homer rubbed his chin. "Or supposin' that busy body Campbell guy up the road got antsy 'bout all the crew traffic and complained to someone."

Gerald handed the binoculars back to Homer. "Let me know if there's any more traffic. I'll tell Jake at the lab to hold the crew for the next hour or so. In the meantime I'll be at the lab with Becky and the Gordons. We're not far from completion, Homer. We can't blow it now."

"Care for some coffee?" Hal asked Broils sitting across the desk from him.

"Something stronger would be better, but coffee will do."

There was a pause while Holtz poured the coffee into two Styrofoam cups and returned. He settled down at his desk and sipped his drink. Broyles leaned toward him.

"What's this about the CIA?"

"Apparently our headquarters in Chicago got a call from the city's CIA office. They were very vague about the whole subject but asked some questions along the lines of yours earlier today. They never mentioned the Purdue Raisbeck thing, but they did suggest that Purdue was involved in some highly classified project and wanted to know if we knew anything about it."

"That's a switch for those guys. Normally, they go their own way, to hell with the FBI."

"They talked to a guy named Manning—like the Colts Quarterback."

"He's my contact in Chicago. We worked together on the Pence kidnapping and his wife's murder. What did he tell them?"

Hal took another sip of coffee. "He said nothing! He pleaded complete ignorance."

Broyles smiled briefly. "Manning's pretty cagey, but I'm sure they must have had further conversation."

"Not according to Manning. The call lasted about two minutes.

Broyles finished his coffee, stood up, and slipped on his coat. Hal joined his walk to the door.

"The CIA gang is a persistent group, so we'd better do Whatever we have to to stay ahead of them."

Hal nodded. "Tell me. Is this damn aircraft we're all worried about that good?"

"If this guy Pence is as much of a genius as he seems to be, we'd better get our government involved. Whoever has this craft will rule the skies—and maybe even the world."

He started through the door and turned back. "Keep that gated farm under surveillance. If that other car was the CIA, they're further ahead of the game than we want them to be."

Two days earlier, the Voice had instructed Atkins to meet him at Bruno's Restaurant in West Lafayette at 10:00 a.m. sharp.

"How will I recognize you?"

"Don't worry, I know what you look like." Puzzled, Atkins clicked off.

He sat at a table by a window at Bruno's. It was ten o'clock straight up and down. A tall, thin man entered the restaurant, hesitated a moment, and then approached Atkins's table. He slipped into the seat across from him.

"You're punctual," Atkins remarked.

"One of the elements of success, Mr. Atkins. The other is to simply show up."

"I recognize your voice," Atkins said as he leaned toward the man. "You shaved off your mustache."

"Indeed. We met in Quebec. Let me introduce myself. My name is Charles Manning. I'm an FBI Special Agent from Chicago."

"FBI!" Atkins almost shouted. "Good God, am I under arrest?"

"On the contrary, Mr. Atkins. For the last several weeks you have been working with our organization. That is, of course, if you give me the information I asked for."

Atkins withdrew a notebook from his coat pocket. "As a matter of fact, I can. Two days ago, I nosed around like you suggested after I got to this place. On a hunch, I parked in front of the FBI office here. Shortly, what I assume was an agent came out, got in his car and after studying a slip of paper, drove off. I followed him." He tore a page out of the notebook and slid it across to Manning.

"It's all here. A farmhouse south of here. With all the traffic when I got there, I was sure I had hit pay dirt."

Manning studied the note and looked up with a broad grin. "Well done, Atkins. How do you propose to abduct the girl?"

Atkins, in the process of sipping his coffee, gagged.

"Oh, no! I've done more than I should for you guys! If you want that girl, you can get her yourself!"

Manning leaned back leisurely. "You forget, sir. You are wanted for suspected homicide. I could handcuff you right now."

"Bastards—all of you!"

Atkins looked toward the door. Maybe he could make a run for it.

"Don't try it, Atkins. You'd never get to your car."

Atkins sat back in resignation. "Okay, what is it you want me to do?"

"Use your initiative the same way you did at the FBI office here. Find out if Miss Pence is truly at the farm, and if she is, somehow get her in custody. If you're successful, Atkins, we'll forget that we ever saw you."

Atkins smirked. "What's to keep me from taking off from here?"

"I suggest you don't try it."

Broyles returned to his office in Indianapolis and called Manning. For a change, he was there.

"Have you heard the news?" Manning inquired.

"No. What is it?"

"That Upstein nut tried a jail break in a helicopter this morning."

Kyle Broyles changed ears. "He what?"

"As I understand it, his second appeal was denied last Thursday, and I suppose he decided to arrange for a break-out through his attorney, who is now being held as an accessory. In any case our attorney friend, Berman, hired a helicopter to swoop down and grab Upstein during morning exercise."

"Are you kidding me?"

"Unfortunately, the helicopter pilot was not aware of telephone wires in the area and he crashed, killing himself and three other prisoners including Upstein. It's all over the media."

"My God!" was all Kyle could say. There was a long pause, "Well, I guess that closes that case," he finally offered.

Manning said, "Aaaaaaaand, we think we know where Pence is hiding out."

"Hell, that's what I was calling you about!"

A chuckle from Manning followed. "A dirt road south of West Lafayette, a gated farm, a farmhouse, and a barn with a silo."

"Yes, yes. How the hell did you know?"

"I have my sources"

Broyles voice hardened, "And I suppose you know that the CIA has entered the picture!"

"I heard as much, and to me, it makes no difference how our government winds up owning this state-of-the-art thing, or who gets the credit."

"Whoa! What's with you, Chuck? Did you know all this before I went up to West Lafayette?"

"No"

Kyle was now highly irritated. "I thought we were working on all this together, Chuck. Now you're holding out on me. Who is this 'source' you're talking about?"

"I can't tell you now. But we should know something for sure within the next day or two."

Kyle came close to hanging up on Manning, but held back. He took a deep breath and calmed down.

"What is it we will know?" he asked in a controlled voice.

"Where Pence and his daughter are and where this experimental aircraft is being assembled—if, in fact, it is, and where the plans for it are."

"This source of yours, was he up in that area on the dirt road?"

"Yes, he was."

"Son of a bitch!" Kylee hung up.

Gerald, Becky, Steve, Steven Jr., Robert, and Janet sat around the newly fed fire in the fireplace in the farmhouse parlor. They had returned from their tour of the hidden lab.

"I got to hand it to you, Robert. Old Purdue has done you well," Steven Jr. joked.

"More than coloring books in the library, heh?" he answered.

They all chuckled.

"Seriously, Gerald, I never really believed this whole thing would come this far," Steve voiced.

"The way things have been going the last couple of days, I'm not sure I'm happy about the whole project."

"What do you mean?" Steve asked.

"I've invented a Frankenstein! The FBI is on my tail, and I suspect several other entities are tagging along. The Altair is too much for the world right now. Whoever winds up with it will sooner or later use it for evil causes. I have half a notion to blow it up and forget the whole thing!"

Anna walked in with a tray of hot chocolate and passed the cups around.

"Enjoy, folks. It's going to be a chilly night, so load up." She smiled and left the room.

They sat quietly blowing on and then sipping the hot chocolate.

"I hope you're kidding," Becky said. "After all this work, you wouldn't do that, would you, Dad?"

Steve said, "Certainly not before you test the thing!"

"If all goes well tomorrow, I'll be taking it up tomorrow night," Gerald responded.

The group, to a person, bolted upright.

"At night?" Steve questioned.

"There's too much traffic on that road out there," Gerald explained, "I don't want anyone to see the takeoff procedure."

"I'm frightened." Janet moaned.

"Don't be." as Gerald kissed her on the forehead.

With the arrival of the additional guests, sleeping arrangements were changed. Steven and Robert slept in one room, Gerald and Steve in another, while Janet and Becky were assigned a room of their own. They all retired to their rooms except Steve and Becky, who sat silently for a while, staring into the fading fire. Steve spoke first.

"There's a beautiful full moon out there tonight. Let's wrap up and take a short walk."

"I'd like that."

They put on warm clothes and went out into the cold night. The brightness of the full moon lit the area almost to daylight. They walked down the hill from the house and up the driveway toward the gate.

"Do you think you'll ever remarry, Steve?" Becky asked in a tenuous voice.

Steve wasn't expecting the personal question, so they walked farther before he answered. "Carolyn was a wonderful wife and mother. I loved her dearly. She made marriage a great experience for us both."

They walked almost to the gate. Steve continued. "Yes, I'd try it again in honor of that marriage. Carolyn would have wanted it that way."

Becky slipped her hand into Steve's as they reached the gate. "I hope you didn't mind my presumptuous question. I . . . I guess I had to know . . ."

Steve finished her sentence. "If, maybe, you had a chance?"

They turned toward each other, staring deeply into each other's eyes.

"I have a confession to make," Steve said softly. "When I first laid eyes on you last fall, I think I fell for you. I know I was married, and happily so, but I think I fell for you anyway."

She squeezed his hand and smiled. He cradled her face in his hands.

"Whoever wrote that song, 'Moonlight Becomes You,' knew what they were talking about." He drew her to him, and they kissed.

Becky tip-toed into the bedroom hoping not to disturb Janet, but she was awake.

"How was your walk?'

"Most enjoyable." Becky began to dress for bed. "Steve is a very charming gentleman."

"Not a complete gentleman I hope," Janet joked.

Becky crawled into the other bed, fluffed her pillow, and lied down. There was a long silence and then Janet whispered.

"Becky, are you awake?"

"Yes."

Janet flipped toward Becky and rested on her elbow.

"Ever since last fall, I've been worried that you might be resentful of your dad's and my relationship."

"Heavens, no!" Becky smiled. "In fact, I've never seen Dad happier. You've done wonders for him."

Janet rolled on her back. "That's such a relief, Becky."

There was silence for a while. Becky suddenly sat up. "I'm not sure I'm going to get used to calling you Mom, if it comes to that."

They both laughed.

More silence followed. They both stared at the ceiling deep in their own thoughts. Janet spoke. "Do you mind if I ask a personal question?"

"No, go ahead."

"Are you in love with Steve?"

Becky thought for a while and then turned her head toward Janet. "I think I am."

"There's an age difference."

"Not all that much."

More silence and then Becky sat up. "I've got an idea! Let's you and I go horseback riding around the farm tomorrow. Homer can saddle the horses for us. It's going to be a long day. It'll ease the tension."

"Sounds great!"

They both rolled over and finally went to sleep.

"Everything appears to be a go, Mr. Pence. We tested the elevator and the barn mechanism last night. It all worked perfectly."

Jake, the laboratory supervisor, and Gerald stood underneath the Altair. Gerald ran his fingers across the surface of the craft.

"This coating—do you think it will work?" Gerald asked.

Jake brightened. "Let me show you something." He walked off the platform to a bank of switches across the room. "Watch this!"

He toggled a switch. The Altair became barely visible.

"The coating on the surface absorbs the lights above it, as you know, Mr. Pence. During the day, when the sun light is absorbed, it will be even more invisible. So, with the stealth capability, we shouldn't have to worry about military intervention."

"Such is the theory," Gerald remarked.

Jake returned to the platform. Gerald signaled to Farid, who was standing nearby and the three huddled.

"Things are beginning to happen around here that are quite alarming. I don't think we have much time left to complete the project, so I'm testing her tonight. I want everyone out of here who's not essential to the take-off. Do you understand?"

"Yes, sir."

"Farid, I want you to clear out all the notebooks in the other room and take them to our Raisbeck room at the university for safe keeping. No one will understand what's in them but you, but I want them secure nevertheless."

Farid nodded.

"Is all the wiring in place?"

"Yes, sir."

"After I take off, regardless of what happens, I want this place totally vacated. I want every living soul off the property and dispersed. Our guests in the house hopefully will have left beforehand. My plan is to push the button from the Altair if I'm able to do it. If not, Jake, you throw the switch from your station."

They shook hands and Gerald disappeared through the passageway leading to the house. He secured both doors and climbed the basement stairs into the living area. Homer approached him.

"That car's back again, Mr. Pence, and there's a guy tryin' to climb over the fence."

"Where are the girls?" Gerald asked.

"Out horseback ridin'. I saddled the horses for them earlier this morning."

"Jesus!" shouted Gerald. He dashed into the parlor and pulled a rifle from a cabinet against the wall. He grabbed a box of shells, and loaded up a clip as he ran back to Homer.

"Homer you go upstairs with your rifle and keep your eyes on that guy. Stop him if he gets too close. If he keeps coming . . . shoot him!"

Gerald ran out the front door, yelling for the women.

Both of them were flushed with enjoyment as they cantered in the open field some distance from the barn.

"I haven't been on a horse since my Girl Scout days back when!" Janet giggled.

"You're riding Sonny Boy like a pro in any case," answered Becky.

They galloped toward the barn, and as they neared it, a man with a beard jumped out from behind a partially open door. He grabbed the reins of Becky's horse.

"Come with me, young lady," he yelled.

Becky's horse reared, and Atkins lost his grip. Janet charged him and smacked his back with her riding crop. As he fell to the ground, he pulled a pistol from under his coat, and aimed it toward both of the women. Just then the sound of a rifle shot rang out from the farm house.

Atkins's body jerked violently and the gun fell from his hand. He lied still on the ground as Gerald ran up.

"I'll take the horses, girls. You both get up to the house."

"What's going on, Dad?" Becky asked hysterically.

"Don't you recognize this son of a bitch?"

"Is he dead?"

"For his sake, he better be."

Homer ran up and nervously asked Gerald, "Did I kill him, Mr. Pence?"

They stood in front of the barn.

"He's still alive, but not for long. Go on back to the house, Homer. Keep your eye on the road."

By this time, Steve had come down from the house. They took the wounded Atkins into the barn and did their best to stop the bleeding. Gerald turned to Steve.

"I'm going to ask you to leave me alone with this guy. I have a few questions I want to ask him before he's gone."

Steve nodded and left.

The parlor was full of expectant people as Gerald entered.

"Everyone have a seat. I've got quite a bit to say."

They all sat.

"First of all, Daryl Atkins is dead. But before he died he told me what happened in the Caymans, about the Swiss bank account, and most importantly, who he was working with after that. He was working with none other than FBI Special Agent Charles Manning."

"He was one of the two agents that toured the park last year," Steve remembered.

Gerald continued. "It's my feeling that the FBI is hot on our trail and it would behoove us to move quickly. You've probably noticed all the cars leaving the farm. All but the essential people have vacated the lab, so after a few minor details, I'll be ready to take off in the Altair."

"But I thought . . ." Becky said.

"You thought it was happening tonight. Well, things have changed. Our friend Daryl Atkins has given me an earful. Steve, I want you to leave with your group right away. I want you to take Becky and Janet with you."

Janet bolted up in her chair. "No, Gerald, I'm not leaving you! Whatever you do or wherever you go, I want to be with you!"

Gerald shook his head. "Janet, I dearly love you, but what I have in mind, I don't want you to be a part of."

"Gerald, please."

Gerald walked over to the fireplace and placed his hands on the mantle. He was momentarily deep in thought. He turned to the group.

"Folks, here are the facts of life. I am now a fugitive from the United States government. I'm wanted for quite a list of criminal violations. I've developed something that the authorities would kill to get a hold of. I've already told you how I regret that. I've got to go where no one can find me or the Altair!"

"Where would that be?" Robert and Steven Jr. inquired simultaneously.

"You don't need to know that. Just do as I ask."

"I will not go!" Janet shouted.

Gerald gave her a hard stare, but said nothing.

"What 'bout the property?" Homer asked.

"It won't be livable here soon. I suggest that you and Anna go back to your home in Elkhart. Your jobs are over."

"What have you done with Atkins?" Becky asked.

"From here on out, he's no longer a problem to anyone. With providence having taken care of Upstein, the slate is completely clean."

"Does that go for me?" Tears rolled down Janet's cheeks as she asked.

"Janet, dear, I don't want to take the chance that this whole thing may literally blow up! Please understand. I love you. That's why I want you to go with Steve."

Janet ran to Gerald and threw her arms around him. She was fully crying. "I love you, and that's why I'm not leaving!"

Gerald shrugged in resignation. He looked over to the rest of the group and rolled his eyes. "I could bind and gag her, but heaven help me if I tried."

"Dad, can't you tell us what you have in mind?" Becky asked.

"No, I can't, honey. Just go with Steve. Judging from what I've seen, you deserve to have the kind of future you'll have with him. Now, before it's too late, everyone! Haul ass!"

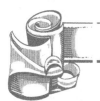

CHAPTER 18

Robert stopped Steve after they left the security gate. "Dad, I've worked too hard on this project not to see this thing through."

Steve pulled the car over to the side of the road where they would have a good view of the barn.

Janet sat to the right of Gerald in the Altair. All preparations had been made. Gerald turned on the aircraft radio.

"We're all set, Jake. As soon as I see you leave the farm yard, I'll proceed."

Jake's voice crackled a response. "Right, Mr. Pence. Good luck."

Gerald looked over at Janet who was looking straight ahead nervously. They then exchanged smiles.

"It's not too late to change your mind, Janet."

"Never!" she shot back and looked straight ahead again.

The LCD showed Jake's car moving down the drive way and through the gate.

"Okay, here we go, for better or worse."

Jake's car pulled in behind Steve and his group. They all looked toward the barn. Minutes passed, and suddenly the barn roof parted at the apex. The Altair appeared on its platform as it elevated above the open roof. The craft rose slowly, cleared the platform and suddenly shot into the sky. Steven Jr. was beside himself.

"It works! The son of a bitch works!" He wrapped Robert on the back. "Nice goin', you old Boilermaker, you!"

The Altair hovered some distance from the barn when, with a mighty roar and a cloud of dust, the barn imploded. At that same moment, the farmhouse collapsed with another devastating implosion. All the witnesses sat spellbound. When the dust settled, what remained were two piles of splintered wood and twisted metal. The Altair disappeared.

After a prolonged silence, Steve said quietly, "Let's go home."

The front pages of daily and weekly newspapers in Chicago, Indianapolis, West Lafayette, Lafayette, and surrounding areas ran as follows:

BARN AND FARM HOUSE DISAPPEAR:
FBI And Local Police Investigate Strange Collapse of Barn and Farmhouse in Central Indiana

The FBI along with local police are investigating the collapse of a barn and farm house in a secluded farming area southwest of West Lafayette, Ind. So far, no fatalities have been reported, and it won't be determined what caused the collapse until wreckage crews have sifted through the debris. The property is registered under the name of a Gerald R Pence of Indianapolis. Mr. Pence was not available for comment.

And carried on the evening newscast of WCHTV in Chicago:

"Jason Randolph is on the scene of a bizarre happening on a small farm in Central Indiana. Come in, Jason."

"I'm standing here by the wreckage of a collapsed farmhouse and barnyard not twelve miles southwest of West Lafayette, Indiana. No one knows what caused the collapses and crews have just begun to sort through the wreckage. There is no report of injuries so far. I'm standing beside Lafayette Police Chief Ernest Downing. Sir, do we know anything at all about what has caused all this?

"Not at all, but this particular farm has experienced some complaints recently having to do with a great deal of road traffic in and out of the property. We don't know if this has anything to do with what's happened here, but I'm sure we'll get to the bottom of this soon."

"Thank you Chief Downing. We'll keep you informed of this breaking news as it develops. This is Jason Randolph, WCHTV, Chicago."

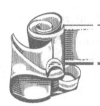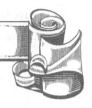

CHAPTER 19

Steve grilled the steaks and made the mashed potatoes. Becky did the rest, to get them all ready for their holiday dinner. Robert was home on break, and Steven was still enjoying his semester off from IU. Doc Ewing accepted an invitation to join them for the meal. Steve offered a suitable prayer, and for the next hour and a half, they enjoyed each other's company with banal conversation. After dinner drinks were served, Steve sobered the evening by asking Doc about his son, Jon.

"I got a letter from him only two days ago. He's still in Afghanistan, but he couldn't say much about what was going on with him. At this point, he seems to be okay!"

"Great!" Steve raised his glass. "We'll drink to that."

Doc reciprocated. "How did your interview with that FBI guy go yesterday?"

"Broyles? He's a nice enough guy. Only doing his job. He asked me about Robert here and his involvement with the Pence thing. I explained that it was only a class project in dynamic aeronautics, and he seemed to be satisfied with that."

Steve took a sip of his drink. "Then I asked him about his cohort, Manning, and his involvement in all this.

He seemed a little reluctant, but he finally told me a very interesting story. After all the activity at the farm and after they found Atkins's body, he said that he rang up the assistant deputy director of affairs in DC and reported the Manning situation. It was a risky thing for him to do. It could have cost him his job, but thankfully, it didn't. He then told me that Agent Manning has been since transferred to a little community in North Dakota where they are developing new oil fields in Wilkerson, I believe he said."

"The boondocks!" Doc remarked.

Gerald nodded his head. "Broyles told me that that whole area is like the old west used to be. In addition to a flood of out-of-work people, there're the gamblers, prostitutes, murderers, and thieves. Its a rat nest environment that will keep Agent Manning quite busy and quite miserable for a long, long time. We shook hands and he left."

"You always were a slicked-tongued son-of-a-gun!" Doc smirked.

They all laughed.

"And what about the bank account in Switzerland?" Doc asked.

"The IRS has been informed, so we can forget all about that."

Doc drained his glass, thanked everybody, and went home.

Robert and Steven had gone into Williams Creek to do some shopping while the stores were still open. Becky and Steve finished the dinner cleanup and now sat on the deck, staring at the quarter moon in a relatively clear sky.

The temperature continued to defy the season at a balmy sixty-two degrees. After a long silence, Becky took Steve's hand. She stared at his well modeled features, his strong chin, and long straight nose.

"Does this bother you, Steve?" she asked in a soft voice. He squeezed her hand and smiled at her.

"Not in the least. I'm a happy man."

"Do you think of her?"

"Carolyn? Of course I do. I think of her and then I'm grateful for how much like her you are."

She leaned over and kissed him on the cheek, then settled back to stare at the sliver of moon.

"I wonder where they are?" she whispered.

"Who?"

"Dad and Janet," she answered.

There was more silence as Steve gave the question some thought. He waved his arm at the sky.

"I think they're up there somewhere."

"In space?"

"Who knows? The machine was capable of sustaining itself indefinitely up there."

"Where would they go?"

"Lord knows. Gerald probably has a plan. But I can't help feeling that we'll see them again . . . sometime."

She hugged him tightly. "I hope so."